ate it anyway

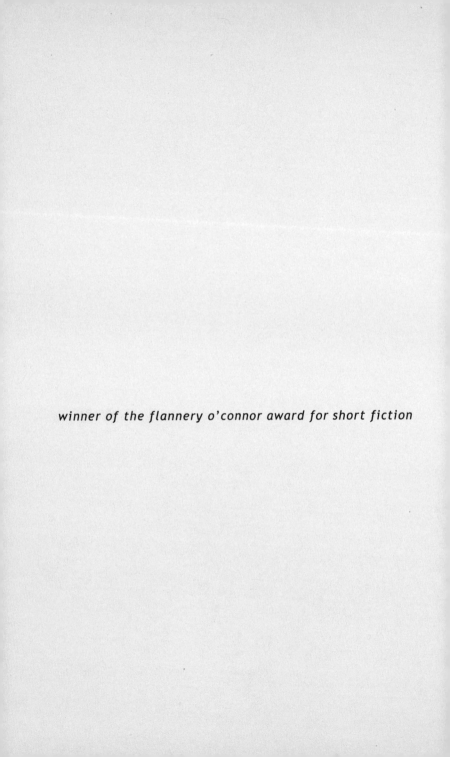

winner of the flannery o'connor award for short fiction

ate it anyway

Stories by Ed Allen

the university of georgia press

athens and london

Published by the
University of Georgia Press
Athens, Georgia 30602
© 2003 by Ed Allen
All rights reserved
Designed and typeset by
Stephen Johnson
Printed and bound by
Maple-Vail
The paper in this book meets the
guidelines for permanence and
durability of the Committee on
Production Guidelines for Book
Longevity of the Council on Library
Resources.

Printed in the United States of America
07 06 05 04 03 c 5 4 3 2 1

Library of Congress
Cataloging-in-Publication Data
Allen, Ed, 1948–
Ate it anyway : stories / by Ed Allen.
p. cm. — (The Flannery O'Connor Award
for Short Fiction)
ISBN 0-8203-2558-9 (alk. paper)
I. Title. II. Series.
PS3601.L425A84 2003
813'.6—dc21   2003008495

British Library
Cataloging-in-Publication Data available

contents

acknowledgments

The stories listed here first appeared, in slightly different form, in the following publications:

"Singing Pumpkins," "Hungry Hungry Hippos," and "In a City With Dogs" (under the title "The Beautiful Ones") first appeared in the *New Yorker.*

"Celibacy-by-the-Atlantic," "Hot Plate," "Ralph Goes to Mexico," "A Lover's Guide to Hospitals," "Night of the Red Palm," and "Ashes North" were published in *Gentlemen's Quarterly.* "Ashes North" was reprinted in *New Stories from the South, 1997.*

"River of Toys" was first published in *Southwest Review* and was included in *The Best American Short Stories, 1990*.

"Burt Osborne Rules the World" first appeared in *Story* and was reprinted in the *Sun*.

"A Puddle of Sex Books" was first published in *Alaska Quarterly Review*.

"A Foolish but Lovable Airport" was first published in *Antioch Review*.

"How to Swallow" was first published in *Boulevard*.

river of toys

I love to walk with my eyes closed. At night, when I come back to my apartment from work, there are almost no cars on the road, and I can walk and walk until I hear a car coming from behind or until I see through my closed eyelids the light of one coming toward me, and I open my eyes and find myself walking in the middle of Highland Avenue.

I love to walk in the middle of the night, past the dark Laundromats, past Kentucky Fried Chicken standing dim in its all night utility lights. With the road empty, the students gone, most of the faculty on vacation, it's so quiet that I can hear the trickle of water where Highland Avenue crosses Fairfax Creek.

I like to close my eyes and think about where I used to live, in Ramapo Bungalow Colony in Spring Valley, New York, and about the water in Pascack Brook, which flows past the bungalows. I like to think that in its three miles, from where it springs out of a patch of wet ground behind the Hillcrest Shopping Center to the place behind the United Parcel Service distribution center where it joins Ramapo Creek to become the headwaters of the Hackensack River, it touches on everything that a neighborhood needs to become the kind of home that remains a home even after you've left it for something better, even during the long remainder of one's life in which one gets stranded for perfectly good reasons away from it.

Pascack Brook begins in a patch of wet ground in the woods behind the Grand Union. It runs into a long pipe that takes it under Wollman Street. It rambles through the front yard of the Hillcrest Retirement Home, into a pond bordered in summer by weeds as tall as a man, runs downhill between the sloped backyards of the newer subdivision houses.

It runs along the edge of a field where somebody has a horse, the grass nibbled down to an even green fuzz. There is a white horse shed and a two-car garage with a wrought iron outline of a horse and buggy on the clapboard triangle formed between the top of the garage doors and the low peak of the roof. And then the brook goes underground again, coming out in somebody's backyard so steep they can't run a mower over it, then down to a flat section where it loops through another subdivision where backyards slope down to it, yards full of toys in bright yellows and blues, wingless airplanes, trucks without wheels.

I have listened to the voices of children playing late into the night on nights when I had to go to bed early for the first day of a new job. I have memorized the placement of rocks in the brook beside my bungalow so that I could balance in the dark, have gone weeks of perambulating twilight reverie without once getting a soaker. I have thrown slivers of cheese product or Steak-umm sandwich meat into the water for the school of chubs who thrashed and splashed around after it, have balanced between two rocks, nearing the end of my unemployment benefits.

A neighborhood is whatever anyone wants to remember about it, a place where the ground is warm under a man's feet, the mud cool, the smell of fresh tar arises from the gravel, and the lights of the Fireman's Carnival filter over the trees on the other side of the high-tension wires. There are teenage girls who drive around in their mothers' Oldsmobiles wearing heavy eye makeup and blouses with elastic at the neck pulled over one bare shoulder, but I'm exaggerating. There was one girl who used to drive past. I wanted to tell her, in complete seriousness, "We couldn't be more wrong for each other; we have nothing in common but the leaves and the heat and the line of a crooked smile and the air like an umbrella of moisture and stars you can't see, domed above my dreams of a relationship that I say will work because we both know it never could; and so by the same implacable gravity that draws the small water in its bends and meanderings through subdivisions where the roots of trees haven't yet grown out of their burlap coverings and the kids play tag into the night from yard to yard, by that same law I say we shall be married, in the month of May."

I like to close my eyes and walk, see how far I can go without opening them. The night has a shape that hangs over everything I hope to get back to, over my going home from work, over the books I tell myself I should be reading. Stars hang in the sky whether you can see them or not, even on nights so humid that people who smoke cigarettes can't light matches.

When the water in Pascack Brook was low, which it usually was, I used to walk every night in the dark from rock to rock with the soft light and the music from WPLJ, the "Stairway to Heaven" flagship station, coming out of my neighbors' rear window, around which the climbing thorns had grown so thick that the tendrils were starting to work their way through the holes in the screen. Whenever there was a heavy rain, you could hear the rocks moving underwater with a muffled blocky sound, and when the water went down, the layout of the stream would be completely changed, with different rocks to stand on, different crossings to remember, providing a rare example of geological history observable within our own lifetime.

I wonder what that girl's name was, so beautiful and cheap in her mother's car. I'll never know. She looked a little bit like a girl named Karen whom I used to be friends with, whose father was my mother's podiatrist and whose house Pascack Brook runs past on its way to the bungalows and the Hackensack River. I want to tell Karen that I'm sorry about all my Rabelaisian remarks around the kitchen table, playing Sorry in the old farmhouse in Blauvelt that summer when nine of us shared the rent. I was like a dog chasing cars who wouldn't know what to do if he caught one.

There is a wonderful temporary nature to the kind of poverty I find myself in this summer. Days are simple; I'm either working or not working. I've written out a budget, and I stick to it, more or less, except on days when the tips from the night before have been better than usual. In the daytime I follow the railroad tracks to work, past the elementary school and the Coors distributor and the Bloomington Elks Club and the municipal swimming pool and the Little League fields. It's so hot that I have to time myself to get there early enough so that I can hang around in the bathroom waiting for the sweat to dry, and I always have to remember to bring my deodorant in my little blue nylon knapsack, along with my black pants and my black shoes and my white shirt and my bow tie.

I love to think about my car and how soon I can get it back from where it sits in the backyard of a garage in Russell, Kansas, where the engine blew up in June on my way out to make a million dollars at a summer job that I had convinced myself I would be able to find in the salmon fishing business. The garage made me leave a two hundred-dollar deposit with them to hold the car until I send the money to rebuild the engine. This left me just enough to fly back here, where I managed to get my job back at the Oak Room, from which I had taken a summer leave of absence.

Although it's the off-season, they are glad to have me back, because now there's somebody to look after things while my boss drives back and forth from University Hospital, where his mother is dying of cancer. So I watch the bar and answer the phone. At least half the people who come into the bar are just asking for directions, for which I no longer have to look at the map or ask one of the other customers, which means, I suppose, that I really live here now and that the layout of the town has become the same as the way I picture it to myself—all the buildings, all the eyes going by in cars, kids making funny faces out the back windows of station wagons, people with expensive sunglasses, the painted eyes of girls in their mothers' cars, a party of luminous faces around the fluted glass candle dish that shines in the center of each table in the lounge as I pad back and forth in my black shoes on the rubber mat in the orange light.

I am saving up my money, working as many nights as they ask me to, and doing elaborate mathematical calculations—about how much I'll have in the bank three weeks from now, about whether the night is five-eighths finished or closer to three-quarters, about how much money I will have saved by the time I've lived here long enough to be an official in-state resident and I can enroll in the university at a lower tuition, which is what I came out here for in the first place.

Right now I have a crush on one of the waitresses, a girl whose face catches the light in the soft way that the kind of light they put in cocktail lounges was designed to do—one of that class of Army daughters from so many different places at once that she seems to have sprung, fully formed, from a generalized, nonregional landscape. Her boyfriend lounges in the bar every night, waiting for her to get off work. He is so laid-back that once, when I asked him how his glass bric-a-brac business was going, he couldn't work up the energy to tell me, just looked away slowly and settled back in his chair, filtering Heineken through his black mustache as if extracting krill.

I have discovered a rule by which the personality of the future husband varies in inverse proportion to the attractiveness of the future wife. In the meantime I answer the telephone, waiting at each ring for the inevitable news, at which time we will hang black bunting—which they have already shown me where it is—over the front door and close for a few days.

Going home, I love the smells of the night, the murky green pollen of the weeds that grow at the places where Fairfax Creek runs under Highland Avenue, the barely perceptible undertone of dead animals, the sweet lampblack of exhaust from cars that aren't running right, the carbon dust that hangs over the street long after most of the traffic has gone home. Sometimes cars go by with gasoline splashing out from underneath their license plates. I remember one night in the pouring rain when Pascack Brook had somehow become filled with gasoline, and the smell was so strong that my neighbors sitting on the porch were afraid to light their cigarettes. We called the police. When they came I walked out into the rain to speak to them. The smell had already started to go away. The two cops and I stood on the inclined slab of concrete beneath the floodlight at the edge of Bungalow C and watched the brown water speed past in the bright light, full of leaves and branches. They said to call back if the smell got strong again, and then they left, and since I was wet already I just stood there watching how the water would sluice past over a continuous wave in front of where I stood listening to the rocks clunking together on the bottom.

When I lived in the bungalow colony I used to call the police all the time. At two o'clock in the morning a school bus was roaring around the neighborhood, barreling up and down the silent streets. It seemed very suspicious, so I called the police. A dog was trapped in the woods on the other side of the power lines, with his leash snagged in the crook of a tree, so I called the police. A red-bearded derelict was walking back and forth all day along Pascack Road; a very large, dead, gray tiger cat was lying by the road, his belly bloated, stinking up the whole neighborhood. For some reason the sanitation department was not in the phone book, so I called the police. I would have buried it myself—I had nothing to do—but it's not my job. There are people who get paid to pick up dead animals.

I suppose you could call it a river despite its small volume of water, because it follows the dentings of the land, and the title abstract companies recognize it as a border between properties, some of which have been on the town map for generations. It's always in the same place, and it's always there in the morning, except for the one summer when it dried up completely. A school of chubs, trapped in a pool that my neighbor Dominick had built by piling rocks into a dam, swam for a day with their mouths at the surface of the oxygen-less water, and the next day they were all dead.

In the patch of woods where it begins, where kids from Cameo Gardens have cleared an oval track where they ride round and round on their bicycles, jumping roots and rocks, it springs from a little puddle, forming a trickle of water no larger than what a garden hose would give forth if you were trying to fill a dog's dish without splashing. There in the woods, bright with cans and bottles and license plates not old enough to be worth collecting, a path runs from the bicycle track to the edge of the parking lot, where you're not supposed to work on your car but everybody does anyway, and there is a sort of window in the foliage and a black pit in the dirt where people from Cameo Gardens dump the used oil from their cars. I suppose you could say that the water is born dirty, like a child born with its mother's virus.

Across the brook from the bungalow I used to live in, there stands a cement cone four feet high, connected to some sort of waste conduit that runs parallel to the brook, a rounded shape that rises from the weeds like a tiny volcano or an African anthill, with a round iron lid cast in a crosshatched pattern like a mint wafer. In summer there comes from that conduit some nights a thick odor full of methane and phosphorus, something old and rich and rounded at the edges, steaming out from underground.

I have found so many toys washed downstream in Pascack Brook that I always had something to play with in the days when I was collecting unemployment insurance. I found plastic sand trowels and water-powered rockets. I found so many toys in Pascack Brook that the kids who lived upstream from me must have been thought fools by their parents. I have found toy cars, toy helicopters, submarines, an army truck full of drowned soldiers, one with his head knocked off. I have found balls: volleyballs, spaldeens, waterlogged softballs, Wiffle balls, a hollow ball for dogs, with bells inside it, a blue and black and white ball that if I spun it on the floor looked like the planet Jupiter, and another that looked almost exactly like the Voyager photos of Jupiter's moon Ganymede. I have found armless dolls drowned against the gridwork of abandoned Waldbaum's shopping carts. For some reason people always throw shopping carts into the water, and they roll downstream with every big rain, ending up wedged between boulders, like ruined lobster traps, twisted, covered with algae, bits of chrome shining through the rust, their caster wheels pointing up in the air and snagged at the hubs with tufts of dried grass.

I have bounced tennis balls with the nap worn off them against the walls of my bungalow and wondered how far upstream they originated, if they have passed, rolling in the dark water, beneath the windows of the house where my friend Karen used to live. Now she's in Colorado, married to some guy I've never met, whose personality I can only assume fulfills the usual algebraic requirement of inverse proportionality. But then of course Colorado is so beautiful that it doesn't matter; you can be the most boring person in the world and nobody will notice. I apologize for all the jokes about your breasts, there at the Sorry table, but even if you were still around, that would be all over now; my doctor says I have to give up half my sex life, and I have to choose which half: thinking about it or talking about it. All I know is that loving you has made me a better person—look! Peter had a picture of you naked, that summer at the farmhouse, standing in a field, your back to his Nikon. I used to turn the picture around and hold it to the light to see the front.

I was sorry to hear that your father died. I would have sent a card, but those cards are strange, and it's strange to think that the person who died hadn't even gotten sick yet when the card was written.

He was a nice man, a bit silly. He did wonders for my mother's feet. His nickname for you was "Pussycat," which he had the unfortunate habit of shortening to just "Pussy," and he could not be made to understand, or you could not bring yourself to discuss with him, the vulgar meaning of that word, hence your embarrassment that day in the Goodyear Service Center when the car was ready and your father called to you from the service desk into the waiting room, "Pussy! We're going home now. Pussy!" and all the way up and down the six bays of the service area, the mechanics were laughing so hard that the wrenches fell out of their hands and clanged on the floor.

What can I say about the dirty water that won't make me sound crazy? I'd like to walk in it and let the water run all over me, as it ran over that little kid, according to my neighbors who had been in the bungalow colony for five years when I moved in, the kid from the federal housing project up on the hill who drowned in the brook and whose body washed under the wooden bridge leading from Pascack Road to Eden Acres and rotted there for weeks until the skull floated free and some kids found it. I would like to spend a whole day waxing nostalgic for that water and maybe even squeeze out a tear, because it would feel good, and I read in *Psychology Today* on the plane back from Kansas that tears contain a kind of protein that the body is trying to get rid of. And when my body has gotten rid of enough of that protein, that means that I will be good at whatever I do, and I shall have my master's degree, and I shall be able to fly back for a weekend without having to worry about all the things I've let myself get behind on to get there. I shall buy knee-high wading boots for sloshing upstream on the slippery green rocks. I shall rent a midsized car at the airport. I shall start at the ocean and follow the water upstream by whatever roads run closest to it, from the Verrazano Narrows Bridge, where you can look east from the roadway into the open sea, and then north along the edge of Staten Island, overlooking the supertankers riding at anchor in the Upper Bay, then to Bayonne, along Newark Bay, through Jersey City, and up the mighty Hackensack, all the way to Hackensack, upstream through Westwood and Hillsdale, to Woodcliff Lake, beside my favorite restaurant, the Golden Musket, where in the middle of the day fierce geese with bulbous red knots on the bridge of their bills honk and hiss at the drivers from the food service companies, to Pearl River, to Nanuet; and there, where the Hackensack River begins, at the confluence of

Pascack Brook and Ramapo Creek, overlooked by the window-less blond brick of the UPS building, so new that no grass grows on the dirt sloping down from it, at that confluence, where any toys that have rolled this far downstream will sink to the bottom and never come up, there stands a flat rock, and upon that rock I say I shall stand and look downstream to all the places I have never been, shall build my dynasty of one that goes back as far as I want to say it goes back; I bid you welcome, lovely ladies, kind gentlemen. The name of my house is "Falling Water."

celibacy-
by-the-atlantic

It was a clever idea, but the movie did nothing with it. The noncheerleader girls, wearing their boyfriends' leather jackets and popping gum in time to the music, swaggered between rows of combination lockers and advanced toward the camera in a phalanx of lipsticked smiles. Phil Heath sat in his wooden folding chair, his rear end already getting sore. He kept noticing how the girls on the screen, with their bell-shaped hair set a little too high on their heads, looked as if their saddle shoes wouldn't be enough counterweight to keep them from tipping over.

"You want to leave after *five minutes*?" This was Phil's older sister, Gwen, her eyes widening in the screen's light, glaring at Phil with the same look of mock astonishment she had been giving him ever since they were teenagers, whenever she thought he was being stupid.

"This is dumb, Gwen. I'm bored."

It was the weekend of the island's annual Winter Festival, when stores reopened and summer people flew back for three days of half-price shopping, along with concerts by the Providence Pops, guided tours of the island's oldest houses, and classic film festivals. For the Heaths it had become a family tradition: to browse for hours in soap-scented gift shops, to drive along the beaches and dune trails in the old four-wheel-drive Mazda Phil's parents kept year-round at the house they owned on the north shore of the island.

The only problem with the house was that everybody had to sleep dormitory-style, family and houseguests crammed together upstairs in the unpartitioned loft, where even husbands and wives were expected to refrain from any activity whose overheard noise would embarrass the grown-ups and confuse the children. Thus the cottage had acquired such nicknames as Mariner's Monastery and Coed Convent.

"You're bored?" Gwen said. "After five minutes?"

"I was bored after one minute."

"Well, I wish you'd been the one to stay home with the kids," she said. "Then Mom could have come with us."

"I'm sorry."

* * *

Phil had flown in by himself this year, so the mandate about celibacy on the north shore didn't bother him. Usually his wife came along, but Beth was up in Killington, Vermont, this weekend at a corporate retreat. General Electric was conducting a series of middle-management workshops combined with a program of ski clinics by Frantz Klammer and all this filled out by a cuisine supervised by an associate chef flown in from Spago.

The last time Phil and his wife had been on the island together, Beth was in one of her unpredictable playful moods: she had kissed him good night about twenty times, there on the old-fashioned dormitory bed with the mattress resting on a mesh of steel springs, with Gwen's two kids in their bed five feet away—whether asleep or not they couldn't tell—and on the other side the congested slumber of their father's old Princeton roommate. Phil had lain awake for an hour after Beth had fallen asleep, her warm body gravitating against his in the centripetal sag of the bedsprings and the July breeze whistling through the screen and the beacon from Winnetuxet Light flashing in the window every twelve seconds.

He couldn't get to sleep that night. He remembered even thinking that he might undertake the ultimate act of nostalgia, as he had so many times in this same house over so many summer vacations, silently, under the covers, hoping nobody heard him—but instead, finally, he went padding down the stairs for his Dalmane.

On the film-festival screen, outside one of Springvale's three competing malt shops, the hero (differentiated from his companions by being neither pimply nor fat nor comically large in the Adam's apple) twisted his Marlboros in his T-shirt sleeve, leaned against the caramel fender of his '57 Chevy, and gave his hair two lubricated passes with a comb. Music swelled; the chrome points of the Chevy gleamed. The hero began to sing to his prospective girlfriend, in the old "Unchained Melody" chord rotation of tonic, sixth minor, fourth, dominant. The song he sang addressed the issue of what a paradise this world would be if she would only allow him to kiss her lips. This was the point at which Phil stood up, pulled his new windbreaker from the back of his chair, and began to squeeze sideways past the cramped legs of Gwen and her husband, Eliot. He worked his way toward his father in the aisle seat.

"I'll meet you at the car," he said quietly over the music. None of them whispered; Phil's family had always preferred a sort of low murmur to the hissing whisper that most people use in theaters.

"I can't believe this," Gwen said. "It's just *started*."

"I wish it hadn't."

Phil's father spoke up from his aisle seat. "I thought this was your kind of music."

"Not when it's arranged by Paul Williams."

"Well I think you're really being a bore," Gwen said, her face illuminated by a moment on-screen in which the muscles of the hero's chest were shown in close-up under his snow-white T-shirt. She rolled her eyes upward, then turned back to the shine of Chevy fenders and Brylcreem.

* * *

Outside the theater, which doubled as the gymnasium for the Island Tennis Club, a mild breeze blew in off the water. Along the brick sidewalk, couples strolled after dinner at Call Me Ishmael, window-shopping among the graphics galleries and candle shops and confectioneries, walking their desserts off as they took the long way back to their bed-and-breakfast rooms.

Ever since they picked him up at the airport that morning, Phil had been so thoroughly surrounded by his family that he found himself looking forward to the times he had to use the bathroom. All afternoon, cooped up by the rain, they had huddled around the kitchen table playing Trivial Pursuit, with Phil winning again and again until Gwen had to stop to help their mother with dinner. All that afternoon, Gwen's remarkably quiet kids had sat in a corner, absorbed in their Smithsonian Institution "Whales and Walruses" coloring books, of which Gwen had managed to buy the last two remaining copies on the island.

So he sat there very slowly packing up the game board. He would have liked to go upstairs, but one of the house rules was that you couldn't go upstairs while anybody was cooking or eating because sand would filter down between the cracks in the floor.

Once that afternoon he tried to go outside, but before he could even get to the bottom of the wooden stairway leading from the house to the beach, his jeans were soaked. Later they piled into the Mazda, all seven of them, and his father drove along the outer beach of the island, while his mother clutched the dashboard, as she always did, saying "Honey . . . honey . . . you're going to get stuck!" The car still had a fishy smell to it, from last summer, when they had taken their own garbage to the island dump and one of the garbage cans leaked fish-cleaning residue from its rusted bottom.

Phil zipped up his new blue-and-white parka, which he had picked up at half price this afternoon at Dockside Toggery. The weekly *Lighthouse-Republican* had already declared the Winter Festival a success. Even at night the streets were humming with shoppers; the restaurants—Scrimshaw House, Nor-Easter, Topgallant—were dishing out balsamic flounder and pesto, and, of course, the chowder pots were steaming, at $4.95 a bowl.

* * *

Phil was trying to make himself believe that he'd walked out on the movie because it was so bad, because the director had located all its phony nostalgia in a sort of ghost territory where you couldn't ever tell exactly what year it was, all the famous songs of the decade all together at the top of the charts, all the Chevies and Marlboros and poodle skirts and oiled pompadours jumbled into one bogus, generic, unspecified non-moment.

This was all true, of course, but it would be a fake excuse. He actually walked out because he had been watching the face of the girl the hero was singing to, the giant wideness of her eyes, the dewiness of her lips. He knew that they would soon be kissing—a long, slow, open-jawed embrace, in which you would see the hidden motion of tongues traced from within on the contours of their cheeks.

This was the thing he'd always had a problem watching. The problem was that it made him feel like an idiot. Even now, at 38, with a good house and a wife prettier than most of the girls in the movie (and who he was reasonably confident was not being seduced by some GE middle-management type over the hot mulled wine), even with his own business and good shoes and the best half-price Ralph Lauren windbreaker on the island—still after twenty-five years, whenever he watched anyone else kissing, Philip Heath felt like a dork.

Which was a word they didn't have the first time he felt like one. Back then he would have felt more like a "weenie." Or a "spaz"—that was the word. A cruel word, with that ticklish little buzz at the end: *spaz,* like a fly caught between the window and the screen.

That's what Phil remembered best about this island: the way it felt to be fifteen years old and to watch people "make out," another important term, a solemn expression. People talked about it all year at prep school. People wrote to their best friends about it. Their whole lives, their whole summer, shrank down to one long strategy.

So many times on this island, riding around with no seat belts in somebody else's father's Jeep, or at parties, checking his watch for his eleven o'clock curfew, with Woo-Woo Ginsberg on WBZ playing Gene Pitney or the Shangri-Las, or just when he was in town for that shapeless, formalized, crucial business of "hacking around," Phil would turn out to be the only one not part of a couple, the one therefore whose job it was to find another station on the radio when one of those marshmallow songs by Andy Williams or the Percy Faith Orchestra came on and everybody else was too busy making out to do anything about it.

And then there were the few times he did get lucky. One night, in whatever year the Beatles' "Paperback Writer" was on the radio, there he was, unaccountably, walking with some girl from Emma Willard who was a houseguest of a friend's sister, along Water Street to the edge of town and out to the stretch of road between the West Jetty and Spouter's Bluff where you could look across to the lights on the other side of the harbor, where everybody's parents were sipping martinis behind picture windows in houses to which nobody ever brought their televisions.

There was always that hurry-up factor: how late it was in the year, how soon he had to go back to the Gunnery and she had to go back to Emma Willard. All the time, the night went *boom-boom* in his ears and the time shrank. They sat on a hewn timber running parallel to the path that led down to the water, careful not to give each other splinters. A steamer pulled out between the jetties, white, all lit with white light, heading back to the mainland with its load of Wagoneers and Ranch Wagons and deeply tanned families who had not begun to worry about skin cancer.

And then they were making out. None of that slow stuff, the way people kiss in the movies now, that tentative way they tilt their faces to find the perfect angle for their lips to brush against each other. At the age they were then, you never knew if somebody was going to come along and tell you to get off their property. They kissed and kissed and said nothing, having already exhausted the topic of which people they knew at each other's schools.

There was a protocol about breasts, especially if you were a gentleman from the Gunnery; at the same time, that voice in the back of your head was always yelling at you: "How far can you get tonight?" In the course of reaching around her, you might let your hand brush lightly against her sweater, and the next time you might leave it there and wait and see if she took your hand away.

And all the time that voice would be asking "Is this it? Is this the night?" If so, the kid was always prepared. Phil, wearing clothes he had to buy out of his own allowance because his parents refused to pay for anything so tacky as tab collars and white Levis. Over the long summer, his "protection" had traced a pale ring onto the brown leather of his wallet; when he and his friends went to town on their hacking-around expeditions, they took care always to wear their wallets protection-side-out, with the miniature doughnut shape outlined in the patch of their hip pockets.

Inside her blouse, on her ticklish belly, everything was warm. Or maybe this was that other girl who wouldn't even let him unbutton her sweater. She said she was cold. All he could remember for sure was how warm the lights were in the picture windows shining above them, on the high ground, in the martini houses.

He could have bought one of those places. Ten years ago, before he got married, he had looked at one, a two-bedroom overlooking the harbor, for $80,000—probably worth half a million today. He'd almost made an offer, but then he backed out.

* * *

Phil had an hour left until the movie got out. He walked through the fan-shaped apron of white light outside Anchor Pharmacy, where on a summer Sunday the line for the *New York Times* stretches all the way down to the Fisherman's Museum. This was the same soda fountain where Phil and his friends used to hack around. Hacking around, for all its gravity, was pretty mild stuff. Basically, it meant smoking Newports and laughing a little louder than usual, never anything nasty. They were prep-school kids after all, and they hated any real troublemakers (who never came to the island anyway), hated the kind of "hoods" that tonight's movie was pretending to celebrate. They would walk around in groups of three or four, cigarettes "cupped" in their backward-facing palms, the style they had all learned at school, when they walked along the road into town and had to be prepared if one of the masters drove by.

It was getting colder. Phil realized he had left his hat in the car. He turned down Beaufort Street, walked past the Captain's Wine Rack, hunching down slightly into his new blue-and-white parka. It felt particularly good to huddle against the cold inside such a tight-seamed work of design, with the multiple zippers cutting across the white weave and a dark gray collar folding over and that peculiar symmetrical shapelessness that you see in well-made sportswear, as in the famous photograph of a wind-blown John F. Kennedy walking along the beach near the family compound.

Phil had learned long ago that the right clothes can help you almost as much as being good at a thing. Had he not allowed himself the luxury of custom suits at work, he might not have survived the uncelebrated stress of running his own wholesale office-supply company.

With all the swiveling and reaching he had to do on a bad day, from the telephone to the folders on his desk to the spreadsheet running all day on his Dell, trolleying around on the casters of his chair, sometimes with three people on the phone at once—if he had to do all this while wearing a rack suit from Filene's Basement and feeling the way it would bunch together under the armpits and jam up around the nonfunctional sleeve buttons, he might on some bad day have said the hell with working on his own and mailed his résumé to the New England Stationery Corporation.

* * *

It was the kind of island where people leave their cars unlocked, which Phil was glad about because his father had the keys. As he got closer to the car, he could hear that the engine was on, and he could see the outline of somebody sitting in the driver's seat.

"Well, hello there," his father said when Phil opened the passenger door.

"What happened? You didn't like that movie either?"

The car's heater was running, and the fish smell was stronger than ever.

"Good Lord, that was silly," his father said. "I got sick of it about five minutes after you did." He was wearing his usual island night-on-the-town outfit, appropriate nowhere else in the world but perfect here: a maroon blazer over dark green slacks and a tan thigh-length car coat. It was an old-money look, full of a well-heeled and confident slovenliness, the kind of look that could allow a man who could afford a fleet of BMWs if he wanted them to get away with driving an old Mazda with the fish smell remaining from the time he tried to save the five-dollar garbage collection fee. Phil knew that he could never achieve that look for himself, although sometimes in downtown Providence he did find himself looking in the windows of the Tobby Shop, wondering if maybe one red blazer might come in handy, for Christmas parties if nothing else.

"Well, Dad, we've got an hour to kill. Want to get a beer or something?"

At the Starbuck House they sat in the cocktail lounge, where the vapor of seething milk and steamed fish from the chowder pots rolled visibly across the ceiling every time a waiter pushed through the swinging door between the bar and the kitchen. The lounge was empty except for a large table by the window, crowded with pastel blazers. Phil's father struck up a conversation with the girl behind the bar, whose tag indicated that her name was Debbie.

"Let me guess," he said to her as she poured their bottles of Lightship Lager, the only beer brewed on the island. "I'll bet you're either from Rhode Island School of Design or Cambridge Art Institute."

"How did you know that?" Debbie said with a smile so perfect that Phil remembered he was overdue for his six-month dental cleaning and checkup. "I'm taking a term off from RISD." She pronounced the abbreviation as "Rizz-Dee."

"That's a hell of a good school," Phil's father said to the girl. Except for the ominous dark sun blotches around his lips, Phil's father wasn't bad-looking for sixty-eight—his mouth and chin firm, his eyes not the least bit watery, most of his hair remaining, combed straight back over the freckled scalp.

"So, what do *you* do?" she said.

"That's a flattering question," he said. "Most people ask me 'What *did* you do?'" They both laughed.

They smiled at each other some more and talked about the best restaurants in Providence, and then Phil's father said, "Oh, but I'm being rude. Debbie, I'd like you to meet my son, Phil."

Phil shook hands with her across the bar. She was very pretty, and he couldn't think of a thing to say beyond a slightly ridiculous "Hello, hello." She had the art student's way of making simple clothes look perfect. Over her tight black jeans she wore a floppy jersey, black-and-white striped, and Phil imagined she had measured the width of the stripes to make sure they were wide enough not to blur at a distance, yet narrow enough not to look clownish up close. She had a thin face, but with some softness in it, and her short brown hair brushed against her cheeks when she bent down to wash a glass.

Phil picked Brazil nuts from the bar mix as he listened to his father tell Debbie the story of his career in industrial real estate. He stared off into the bar mirror. His father, that old gentleman with a little too much red in his face, in a tie with whales stitched onto it, had the girl laughing at every joke, and once in a while, she would put her hand on his arm in that weightless, almost pantomimic way some girls have.

Phil could see his own face, flanked by the tall bottle of Galliano, and he knew that some things never change; they just get more expensive. And tonight, as always, on this overmortgaged, overmemorialized island, a place with no history beyond the day the last whaling concern went belly-up—tonight, world without end in a fancy restaurant, Phil was, once again, a spaz.

They had each finished their second Lightship. The bar was getting crowded because the Cherrystone Playhouse production of *Six Characters in Search of an Author* had just let out. Phil took out his wallet, but before he could produce his American Express card, his father, in a gesture smoothed with lifelong practice, flung open his breast pocket billfold, and Debbie made change for a fifty.

Phil did leave the tip, probably too big, but he knew from his one summer of waiter-work, just down the street at the now-defunct Queequeg's, that servers are never insulted by an overly large tip.

"Have a nice night, Mr. Heath," Debbie called after them, and Phil said "Thanks, you too" before he realized that she was talking to his father.

* * *

"You guys should have stayed," Gwen said as their father eased the Mazda over the cobblestones of Water Street, installed two years ago, to much controversy, apparently for no other reason than to be quaint. "It turned out much better than it looked."

The car jounced over the stones. Gwen and Eliot sat in the back and sang as much as they could remember of the movie's theme song: "This is the time of love notes in class / Cokes in the malt shop / Fifteen cents for a gallon of gas / Something something something," and they broke up laughing. They had picked up so much energy from the movie that Phil knew that when they got back to the house they were going to make him play Trivial Pursuit again, and then if he tried to quit they'd start making a fuss about how badly he was beating them. He couldn't do it.

"Excuse me, Dad," Phil said. "Could you let me out? I want to walk back to the cottage."

"Okay, Phil," said Gwen, with a familiar edge to her voice. "We'll quit singing if it offends you that much."

"I don't mind the singing. I just want to walk back."

"It's five miles!"

"Maybe I'll take a cab."

Phil's father stopped the car at the corner of Orange and Barnstable. "Are you sure you know what you're doing?"

"Walking home, I think."

"But *why*?" Gwen said. Cars were slowing down and pulling into the opposite lane to get past them.

"I don't know. I just want to."

He stepped out onto the bricks of Orange Street. "Good night," he said, and as the Mazda pulled away down Orange and the door closed, he could hear his sister pronounce that high, breathless syllable that sounds like *sheeeeeesh*!, which in itself was a piece of nostalgia, because it had been years since he could remember hearing anybody say "Sheeeesh!" Maybe people had been saying it in the movie.

He unzipped his John F. Kennedy windbreaker and walked back into the Starbuck House. The lounge had gotten very busy. Debbie was still at work, but she was out on the floor now, in her perfect stripes, carrying trays of white wine coolers for the post-Pirandello crowd.

She never came down to his end of the bar. He drank a few more Lightships, walking around with the glass in his hand, examining the framed prints on the walls, which represent all the different species of whale that had once been hunted from this island.

* * *

When Phil finally got back to the house, everybody had gone to bed. The only light was in the bathroom, where a hooded night-light was plugged into the socket next to the mirror. In the gloom he could see that the Trivial Pursuit board had been packed away and the table set for breakfast.

He undressed in the dark, then lay in bed listening to everybody sleep: his father's deep respiration, guttural, his mother exhaling with long sighs. When you listen to people sleeping, they always sound as if they're about to die. In the bed next to his, Gwen's kids breathed in a high whisper. The beam from Winnetuxet Light kept lighting up the room as it swept across the window every twelve seconds.

He had been lying still for several minutes, watching the light rise and fall on the strips of insulation nailed between the slanted ceiling planks, thinking of all the nights he had lain awake in dormitories, remembering all the girls he had dreamed about in the dark, when he started to notice a barely perceptible tremor in the floorboards. From the other side of the kids, he heard a muffled grunt that could not be mistaken for one of the somnolent groans he had listened to in this room for so many years. Gwen and Eliot must have thought everybody was asleep. They were failing to be celibate.

All Phil could do was keep still and pretend he couldn't hear them. Meanwhile, out of all the songs in the world he would have preferred to think about, he began hearing the one he had walked out on in the movie, the song where the hero was telling the girl "Imagine if you can / Two castles in the sand / Two dreams that we can share / Your lips will take me there." With all the beer he'd been drinking that night, he became aware that as soon as Gwen and Eliot quieted down, he was going to have to pretend to wake up so that he could go downstairs to the bathroom one more time.

He lay there motionless, watching the room light up every twelve seconds, listening in his mind to that song from the movie, its four chords repeating, and listening to the old breaths and the young breaths and the breaths of his sister getting fucked. He kept reading and rereading the lettering on the insulation strips that had been nailed between the two-by-fours so that every time the lighthouse beam flashed in the window, it said "OWENS CORNING ... FIBERGLAS ... OWENS CORNING ... FIBERGLAS ... OWENS CORNING ... FIBERGLAS ..."

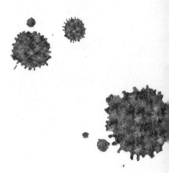

night of the red palm

"One thing I ought to point out is that I don't think morgues are usually ever closed," Chuck said, perched at the edge of his rolling chair and looking down for a minute at the first draft of Kristy Koller's narrative essay and then back up to her face and the red hair around it, stirred, as if waiting to get back out in the wind. "I still don't understand why you say you had to wait for it to be opened."

It was one of those nights on the Sierra State campus when the wind comes down from somewhere that Chuck had never bothered to look up on the map, carrying hot and cold in the same breath, the kind of night when the frond motions of the palms around campus seem to have lost all memory of their tropical tenderness. The dry wind jerks them around in those ocher lights that people's eyes can't quite focus on.

There's no limit to what can happen on these nights. You can run conferences for three hours without having to go to the bathroom. You can even get a student to understand the difference between a thesis statement and a topic sentence.

Kristy stared to the left of his shoulder. She still had her jacket on, a droopy, gray, non-sorority windbreaker. From the ground-level window next to his shared desk, Chuck could see the palm branches flailing around outside, their motions somehow harder to follow when he didn't know any of their species names. Chuck's conferences, on these nights when he had canceled all the day's classes and scheduled another "Chuckathon" down in the adjunct office, usually went so fast that the students didn't need to take their coats off.

Chuck would sip coffee from his Stanley vacuum bottle and swivel in his chair and get them talking about the papers until they got to a point where he could stop them and say, "What you've just said to me right now is much more focused than what you've said in the paper!" and they would nod and understand.

The wind kept up. The palms waved. Green palms, red palms, royal blue, whatever their names are, the kind with a long beard of raggedy brown husks hanging down under the canopy, the pretty kind with a giant wooden pineapple at the top of the trunk, the tall flimsy ones, like dandelions, their flexible stalks, or trunks, standing as high as the array of satellite dishes on top of the Engineering Building.

On a night like this, every hair-trigger car alarm up and down Chapparal Boulevard stands poised, ready to be jarred into life by the shock wave of a passing bass speaker. Every mandatory "Coach's Corner Study Table" ends in a loud mix of laughter and debate about something Chuck can't make out, voices ringing through the halls.

Talk about focus: Kristy's paper was called "The Time My Brother Died." Chuck was so used to making jokes with everybody who came in that he didn't know what to say now except to keep coming back to the morgue not being open.

"That's what I remember," she said, her face blank.

He had learned to trust his instincts about what things to bear down on. There's always some issue in a student paper that provides an instructor with an entrée into its logical problems and by which the student can be made to understand the connections between topic, purpose, context, author, and audience, as shown in the famous molecule-shaped diagram used again and again in the assigned textbook that all the adjuncts used, *Linguistic Strategies for Rhetorical Development.*

On the street another car alarm whooped, warbled, rasped on one note, toggled between octaves, whooped, warbled. Strange to think—looking at things from that bright little adjunct office with so many desks and chairs crammed into it that it looks like a room in a warehouse for used office furniture—strange to think that no matter how hard the wind blows on a night like this, the world goes on. Trim campus patrol officers on bicycles, their helmets a dim half-moon, their taillights flickering red, steer through the blowing dust, prowling for skateboarders. On the opposite side of the boulevard, the little Cushman cart of the Municipal Parking Enforcement Bureau scoots from violator to violator, stricter than ever, now that the grace period has been done away with.

Kristy had a tall face with somehow not much detail to it and long teeth that held her lips apart so that when she wasn't thinking about them, her mouth rested open. The smell of cigarettes drifted from her dark clothes, which he usually hated, but tonight even that wasn't a bad smell, because everything went together, all of a piece—her black combat boots, the casual droop of her coat, her tangled coppery hair, her eyes pale, a drained gray, like a sled dog.

On the side of the filing cabinet next to Chuck's desk, someone had taped a poem, the letters large and grainy from the original being run through the photocopier at the maximum hundred and fifty percent magnification. It was a version of the famous verse by Sierra State's most famous literary graduate.

> *Updated*
> He drew a circle that shut me out,
> Heretic, rebel, a thing to flout,
> But love and I had the wit to win;
> We came back with a gun and blew his fucking *head off!*

Chuck bounced around in his chair, made red marks on the paper. What do you do when you can't make jokes? Two more kids stood waiting for their turn out in the narrow hall lined on both sides with the real offices.

Chuck had found out a year ago that dialing 6617 on the wall phone would make it ring back after ten seconds. Every few conferences, mostly to give his rear end a rest from sitting in that chair, Chuck would excuse himself, get up and dial it, and be almost back to the chair when it rang again.

"Hello?" Chuck would say, a little louder than normal, as the dial tone hummed in his ear and the student looked away.

"You don't say … You don't *say*! You *don't say*!" Then he would hang up, look back at the student, almost begging for the straight line and sometimes getting it.

"Who was that?"

"*He didn't say!*"

He knew he couldn't try anything like that with Kristy, out of respect for the seriousness of her topic. Not that she was crying or anything. This happened three years ago.

Some jokes are so perfect you can run them again and again. Sometimes it's even funny when nobody laughs; it's lonely at the top. Sometimes in front of the worst of his classes on a bad morning, Chuck wanted to do Johnny Carson's old "Tea for Two" desperation soft-shoe up there—but those jokes are still funny, even when you don't tell them, funny down deep into the rhetorical DNA of their own logical structure.

Amazing things: Bugs Bunny. Clean Rest Rooms. You can tell a class that you were almost late because those signs at gas stations kept you busy cleaning restrooms all day. That ancient warm feeling up the back of the spine when they do laugh. But the way they laugh now is nothing compared to the way they would laugh if he could do what he really wanted to do, which was to hold an extra large Magic Marker behind his back and ask somebody: "Would you like your palm read?"

That is the single most perfect joke in the world, though he never actually played it on anybody. You can think about it over and over again, and it stays funny. You can think about it, and for just a second the whole steel-retrofitted building goes crooked, bent but not cracked, all its angles warped into parallelograms. That joke changes everything, sends a tremor out across the dark fields of the republic. Where does that line come from?

That joke is the best sign we have that the world goes on, that the law has not broken down, that there is still something left out there for him to walk around in, as soon as he has finished "conferencing" the students, as the expression goes.

"I know what you're saying," Kristy said. "But I remember they wouldn't let us in until eight o'clock in the morning."

Chuck swiveled in his chair. Sometimes, even with a reasonably good student, you lose an argument. And sometimes you always lose the argument, and you just have to go along with it, but that's not a thought you should ever articulate, even to yourself, because it just makes your job harder.

It was beginning to look as if that morgue was going to stay closed for the final draft. He couldn't say anything, because the only thing he did want to say sounded too much like a joke. He wanted to tell her, "Think for a minute what would happen if they did close the morgue. People die twenty-four hours a day, right? What would the cops do if they found somebody dead? Carry him into the police station and sit him up in a chair?" But every time he thought about how he could word that question, he kept hearing it followed by a rim shot from the drummer.

She could even be called plain but not in the sense of plain meaning homely. Just a slight fringe of blue around her eyes. They come in with these stories, and it's your job to get them to follow the "communication template," so that at least when they have to write a paper for some other class in the future, the teacher of that class won't be firing E-mail messages in all caps to the English department chair. And maybe with a story like this, she can go back to her parents and they will say something like "We're glad you're writing about it, to get it off your chest."

The prettier the girls in his classes got, the milder his thoughts about them became. Chuck used to think that "I Want to Hold Your Hand" was a stupid song, because it asked for so little, but he was learning to understand it better and better. And he knew always to call them *women,* but the word that wanted to roll itself around his throat was always *girl. There's* a Beatles title that was never stupid, that inhaled breath between verses. When the conferences were over, he could take the word to MacGoogleburger's with him, swirl it around the inside of his mouth with beer, and think about the word *girl* as much as he wanted without saying anything, even though the actual faces were becoming harder and harder to keep straight.

She wasn't even the prettiest in the class—third or fourth maybe. And what he was thinking about was just her, the way she was right here, not naked or anything, talking, though not talking very much, waiting to get back outside. Maybe off in the same cartoon universe where you can get away with dressing up like a fortune teller and then slapping people's hands with a paintbrush, she would be crying, the pale eyes pink, the fringe of blue more noticeable in contrast, as if she'd stepped into the bathroom to touch it up, and maybe he would put his arms around her, or maybe just one arm, in that impossible territory, and pull her close enough that they could feel the neglected strength of each other's shoulder muscles.

But if you care about somebody, you're supposed to do whatever you can to help him or her learn to write reasonably coherent essays. And whatever the deal was with not being able to get into the morgue—well, it was three years ago. Maybe what happened was that the morgue was actually open, but there was nobody there with the authority to let them into it.

"Is that what you want me to say?"

"No," Chuck said. "I'll trust your judgment. I've never been to a morgue. If I ever do go, I probably won't be coming back out." (Ba-domp-bomp.)

But it was a troubled paper at best, and it deserved better, especially the conclusion: "G'bye Jim. I'll miss ya, kid."

Maybe it was good that it was three years ago. You don't want somebody crying. But you don't sign off on a paper and just let somebody wave good-bye at the end, even if she means it, even if she loved him, even if the guy was her brother (and that was another part of the problem, he realized suddenly; she never even explained what happened to him); you don't just wave good-bye and then slam the paper shut like a car door. Besides, it was way short of the word requirement. The question is what else interesting can you say about something like this?

"I don't know," she said, but her time was up, beautiful girl. She was already looking out the window at the palms stirring around in the wind near the base of Belltower Hall, where a red light winked at the summit, though any plane flying low enough to be warned by it was already going to crash. She agreed to explain how her brother died and also to punch up the conclusion.

The moment when the conference is already over but the student is still there, gathering up her books and backpack, is always a long moment, because there is nothing more to talk about, except to say have a good rest of the week and see you in class—if she shows up.

She got up, and they said good-bye to each other, Chuck looking to see whose name was next on the sign-up list: not one of the good ones. Before she got to the door, she turned and waved without slowing down, which was a nice thing to do, really. They were always in such a hurry to get out of there that if you were the imaginative type, you might say that the vacuum generated by their departure was what drew the next person in the door with the same motion. She went out so fast, and the next guy came in so fast, that he didn't really need to shout what he liked to shout between conferences, loud as a coach, so loud sometimes that he could hear a fluttering echo from the walls, like what you hear when you clap your hands in an apartment from which all the furniture has been removed. He said it anyway, and she jumped going out, and the other kid jumped coming in.

"Next case!"

wickersham day

Getting the dog off the roof meant that somebody had to pull Danny's Land Cruiser up to the kitchen door, as close as possible to the edge of the house, then Danny would climb on top of the car, while Booger would walk back and forth, not quite understanding that he was on the roof, his long lips swinging, little pink potato buds of squamous cell carcinoma already growing around his mouth.

Danny would call Booger to him over the slanted asphalt, then balance him in his arms before handing him down to Kevin or Michael. Sometimes they forgot to close the door to Laura's room, whose window led to the roof, so that before Danny had even put the Toyota back next to the empty barn, Booger would have stumbled back up the stairs, into Laura's room, and out the open window onto the roof again, barking that shapeless flews-muffled foghorn of a bark out over the blue gravel of the driveway.

On Saturdays and Sundays they used to sit around outside the kitchen in old lawn chairs they had found in the garage, rolling joints in a bread-pan and passing them around as they looked east into the space between the farmhouse and the far subdivisions. Some weekends people's parents drove up to visit, with food and furniture. Danny's mother was the bookkeeper for a home for the developmentally disabled, and she showed them an easier way to calculate each person's share of the rent and the phone bill.

One day, Laura's grandfather came up to the house, visibly frightened. He had just read a book by a psychiatrist named Immanuel Velikovsky, who believed that Biblical cataclysms had been caused by the planet Venus leaving its orbit and halting the earth's rotation—and that these things were going to happen again very soon.

* * *

They painted the kitchen bright yellow. They put up a calendar that Danny had gotten when he took a tour of the Molson Brewery in Kingston, Ontario, on which every day was a different Canadian anniversary that could be celebrated by drinking Molson: Joni Mitchell's first platinum record, the completion of the transcontinental railroad, the establishment of the Hockey Hall of Fame.

So they lived there, sometimes five people, sometimes eight or nine, some moving in, others moving out, cars loading and unloading. At night they stood around in the hard reflected yellow of the kitchen walls. They tried to drink whiskey sours, and they tried to play poker, but they ended up not being able to do either of those things very well. They always ended up with too many things cluttering up the table: magazines, the blender, sour mix, grains of dried sugar stuck to the tablecloth.

Playing poker, at least playing with any seriousness, was hard because they didn't know how to play any of the real poker games. All they knew were games like Cripple Creek Lowball or Upside-Down Pigs-in-the-Chute—usually with fives, suicide kings, and left-handed queens wild. If two or three different dealers named the same game for a few hands in a row, people would start to remember what the rules were, and some nights that would happen, but either way the result was usually the same; people won each other's nickels and quarters back and forth; by house rule no copper was allowed on the table.

A mystery: one day all the food in the house disappeared. Roy drew up a cardboard sign and tacked it on the kitchen door, warning the person not to do it again and saying that the state police had been called, but of course they hadn't. The man who had rented the farm before they moved in had said he was going to have them arrested for supposedly taking away the lumber from a collapsing outbuilding at the edge of the property, and Kevin had to spend an hour on the phone with the state police explaining what it was they hadn't done.

Another mystery: in the middle of a war, in the middle of a dope weekend during which they were celebrating John Diefenbaker's eightieth birthday, a white Lincoln Town Car appeared at the end of the driveway, moving very slowly toward the house. When they walked up to it, the inside of the car seemed as shadowy as the inside of a house with the curtains pulled—the father at the wheel with a hat on, his face old and rheumy-eyed, as he powered the window down.

What he said had something to do either with the fact that the family used to live in the farmhouse and that it made them sad to come back and see it—or that they were just driving around from house to house talking to people out the car window about a woman in Argentina who was about to be made a saint or maybe was one already; from the way this guy spoke, they couldn't tell. He never completely stopped the car, just steered across the blue gravel of the driveway so slowly that you could hear individual stones popping out from under the tires.

* * *

It was theirs only by accident; the ground around the house couldn't absorb water fast enough for the property to pass the percolation test, meaning that the real estate company Danny worked for couldn't get a permit to tear down the house and sub-divide the property. So Danny rented it from them and brought most of his friends up to split the rent.

It had more bedrooms than they would ever need to use, but it was hard to make plans. Nobody knew how long it would last. For some reason it seemed one of those family subjects that nobody wanted to talk about. Kevin seemed to be the only one who ever got worried; maybe the others were on a higher spiritual plane and never had to make themselves nervous thinking about the future. When he tried to bring the subject up around the High-Low Day Baseball table, it suddenly would be his turn to bet or check, all the eyes looking at him, tired of reminding him, and then he would look down at his cards and forget the rules of the game.

Another crisis: The electricity got turned off because the power company had been sending the bills to the real estate company instead of to the house, and the bookkeeper there didn't know what they were for, so he threw them away. Suddenly one Friday afternoon they found out that they owed a thousand dollars. In the candlelight of a long weekend, they sat around telling jokes until they couldn't think of any more. Then they played Sorry, but every time Roy got a good roll, he crowed like a rooster, until nobody could stand to play anymore.

* * *

On another weekend, three of Danny's friends who had just come up on their motorcycles went into town for beer. On the way back to the farm, one of them lost control of his bike and was killed. Nobody back at the house even knew that anything had happened until the kid was already dead and the police called from the local hospital. Danny and Kevin and Michael and Roy and Laura and the two Judys sat around the table that night in the yellow light, not saying much, a quiet night, without poker and without very much beer. Nobody at the farm had ever met the kid who got killed. They sat around trying to understand what it was like to feel sad about somebody whose name you can't remember.

It was sad, but they couldn't sit there and be quiet forever. Later that night, after Roy had gone back upstairs and there was nothing to do but go back to playing Lowball Anaconda Whiskey Barrel—being quieter than usual but not solemn—Danny's dog, Booger, wandered downstairs with a note on a file card hanging on a string from his collar.

"Read it," Danny said, studying his cards.

Kevin didn't want to read it aloud, so he made Booger walk over to where Danny was sitting.

"DEAR MASTER," Danny read, bending down slightly to read the card attached to the dog's collar. "I SURE WISH YOU'D HELP ME LEARN TO STAY OUT OF OTHER PEOPLE'S ROOMS, BECAUSE OTHERWISE I'M WORRIED THAT I MIGHT GET MY FUCKING HEAD BASHED IN."

* * *

Another night, later into the spring, around the dope table, Danny and Kevin spent almost an hour trying to figure out what that day's Canadian reason to drink Molson was, which made it even harder than usual to concentrate on the card game. The calendar had it listed as "Wickersham Day" without explanation. Danny said it just had to be from a cartoon. It was early enough in the evening that the New York Public Library was open. Kevin called to ask, but the person who answered the phone said that they no longer answered people's research questions.

"It has to be something," Kevin said, but it was hard to concentrate over a cookie sheet full of dope seeds rolling back and forth. He kept forgetting to play cards, and it was always his turn to bet, and then he had to go back and figure out whether the hand he held was any good or not and whether or not the queen holding the rose was supposed to be wild this time.

Maybe it was nothing, an instance of a truly Canadian sense of humor. Maybe somebody just put it on the calendar on the least important day of the Canadian year, but it didn't seem that they would make a joke about one of their own holidays.

Just then Roy appeared at the foot of the stairs with a very calm expression on his face, holding a dustpan in his hand, which he tilted gradually until a piece of dogshit dropped onto the floor.

Kevin looked around—a fight, maybe. Everything stood still in the kitchen, the way it does when there is going to be a fight. But there was no fight, just Roy's footsteps softer than usual, up the stairs and slowly down the upstairs hall, to his room, where he did not slam the door.

"Maybe that's what Wickersham Day means," Michael said and laughed at a high pitch.

"I don't get it," Kevin said.

"It means you throw dogshit on the floor."

"I must be stupid. I still don't get it."

Some mornings everybody's toothbrush froze. One weekend Michael fooled around in the barn and managed to get the old

John Deere tractor running. He drove it around the edge of the property several times, letting people sit on the broad seat.

"I'm giving pony rides!" he shouted over the popping bursts of the old two-cylinder engine.

One Saturday everybody got together and tore up the old kitchen linoleum to get to the wide pine boards of the floor so they could sand them and coat them with clear acrylic. The linoleum turned out to have been put there so long ago that the lead story on one of the insulating newspapers under it said that Mahatma Gandhi had been assassinated.

Kevin had a job all spring working in the warm cooking smells of a company that supplied frozen meals to a hotel chain in the Caribbean whose tourist traffic kept speeding up and slowing down. One day they started giving everybody in the plant all the overtime they wanted, and two weeks later half the people got laid off. Kevin walked around the property in the daytime and played poker at night, until he was called back to work again.

In the summer it went for two months without raining. In the fall there was a war. On the day they celebrated Dominion Day—a real holiday that he'd actually heard of—he walked up and down the driveway with the latest news bulletins hanging like ice in his scrotum and wondered what it would look like when the round explosions began blooming to the south.

* * *

No bulldozers came. Kevin got called back to his job twice in the same month, and both times he jumped up and down on the coated wood floor of the kitchen, the way the grand prize winner always did on *The $100,000 Pyramid*.

Instead of the percolation test and the surveyors, something happened that he understood less well. It became harder and harder to get enough people together for a game of Lowball Spit-in-the-Ocean. Fewer and fewer people sat around the table sifting through a bread pan of dope seeds, even on days when there were seeds to sift. Notes on various colors and sizes of paper started appearing around the kitchen, asking people to leave the sink as clean as it was when they got to it or to wipe the crumbs off the table after they had eaten something.

Then one day somebody moved out, and suddenly there didn't seem to be enough gravity to keep the rest of the place from spinning away from the center. Within days, and without anybody planning it that way, everybody that was still living in the house had found other apartments, and all the cars that still ran were being loaded for the trip.

Kevin walked around inside the house, deciding what he wanted to take with him to the place he was going to rent and helping the other people carry things downstairs when they needed it. Nobody seemed angry, not even Roy. They just seemed to be drifting around in a daze, as if there were no more air. If somebody tried to say something, nobody would be able to hear it.

It would have been nice, even this late, to be able to bring up the topic of whether or not it was appropriate to leave notes and what effect notes have on the dynamics of a shared living situation—but since the nature of notes is that they have to be anonymous, talking about the notes in front of other people would have violated the privacy of the person who put them up.

Maybe it was only Roy and one or two others; he never found out. All he knew was that he'd never left a note in his life and never would. Houses need ground rules about notes, which was a thing that Kevin could think clearly about only when it was too late. Somehow, to make a large generalization, notes always lead to somebody's throwing dogshit on the floor. Maybe it would be better in some shared living arrangements if people could on the first day start throwing dogshit on the floor and not have to bother with the long process of notes, but even then it was hopeless. All he knew was that it never works out when people throw dogshit on the floor.

On the last night, Kevin was chopping with a screwdriver in the freezer compartment to help one of the two girls named Judy get some ice trays loose. Her car didn't run right unless it was fully warmed up, so she had it going outside as she carried things around and got ready.

"What's this?" she said, holding a tray under the faucet. She picked a wet file card from the melted frost on top of the tray and read out loud in the quiet of the house:

"BECAUSE NOBODY IS CONSIDERATE ENOUGH TO REFILL THIS ICE TRAY, IT IS NO LONGER PUBLIC DOMAIN. PLEASE DO NOT USE."

"Darling Roy!" she said.

Kevin was about to tell her some of his conclusions about notes, but he decided that even broaching the topic would be itself a little too much like leaving notes, and in this case it would be twice as ridiculous, because they would be addressed to somebody who was not coming back.

Judy steered down the long driveway into the dark, her engine speeding up and slowing down as she gunned it to keep from stalling. Kevin was almost finished loading his own car for the move, but he wanted to stay for a little while, all by himself in the old house. Of all the things you can do in an empty house, Kevin couldn't think of a single one that would have been worth it. You can run around naked or you can break windows, but whatever you do, it's just an empty space, with all the lights on, and dirt all over the place that you will never have to clean up.

What's weird about a note like that is that Roy must have written it months ago. And although it's true that people should refill ice trays and also true that he was probably one of the ones who sometimes didn't refill it, it was strange, and it kept getting stranger, to think that when somebody writes a note, you can still feel how angry that person is even when that person has moved away and is no longer angry.

He promised himself not to bring along any dreary, used broken furniture, even if he didn't have anything else. For the first couple of weeks in his new home, he would be better without such things, even if he had to sit on a flat rock. Two houses don't make a sample, but people had left notes in both the shared-rent houses that he had lived in, and in both of those houses somebody had ended up throwing dogshit on the floor.

In the kitchen, the light was on, bright against the painted walls. Kevin looked and looked. Danny had taken the calendar, so there was no way to tell what Canadian day it was. The only thing he could be sure of was that people all over Canada, and to a lesser extent all over the United States, would be drinking Molson, popping open the ice-cold bottles, but for the first time in months he didn't know what they were supposed to be celebrating. Everything was solid yellow in the light. He flicked the switch and the house was gone.

ralph goes to mexico

Even at highway speed, the Ryder van's automatic transmission seems never to shift, just winds out faster and more frantic, like a washing machine on the spin cycle, revs up from ramp to interstate, to a high whinny at sixty-five. If Lydia tries to go any faster, some kind of governor comes on and literally pushes the gas pedal back up.

In his carrying case on the passenger seat, Ralph cries with what little strength he has left—a dry, lifeless yowl that after listening to it all day yesterday, Lydia hardly hears anymore. Sometimes she pokes a finger through a wide space in the wire door, but Ralph doesn't come toward it.

Interstate 40 seems to concentrate the August light into a sort of hazy tunnel cut into the thick of Arkansas, walls of pine forest on either side of the road broken up now and then by mobile home dealerships, all under a ceiling of blank sky the same color as the white pavement of the road. As she pulls off the interstate into another truck stop, Lydia can feel the allergy shots she got from her doctor in Cincinnati wearing off. In the truck parking area of the Union 76 Truck Plaza, she swallows three Excedrin Sinus with water from her old green wafer-shaped Girl Scout canteen and hides her red eyes behind sunglasses before walking toward the restaurant.

She has left the van running, with the air-conditioning on, to keep Ralph alive a few weeks longer. It idles, dwarfed among the 18-wheelers lined up in a diagonal file from which they can pull out without backing up. Lydia's Mazda clings to the rear of the yellow van, its front wheels mounted up on the towing dolly, its windows piled with the washed whites and maroons of her clothes, most of which are probably too bulky for the heat that awaits her in Tucson.

"So," Dr. Tepper says over the phone, his little voice crisp in Lydia's ear. "Are we eating any better?"

"Not much," she says. "I'm still giving him water and that Nutri-stuff with the dropper."

She sits at a section of the counter where each seat has an individual telephone. The section is marked Professional Drivers Only, but Lydia, who is very good at asking for things, has been given permission to sit here.

She probably didn't need to ask; with her barrel-shaped body and her jeans, which she wears without those fashionable frayed rips in them, she could easily pass for one of the beefy women truckers who are always drinking coffee in these places. The freakish fact that she does not smoke would probably be interpreted here as meaning only that she is in one of those moments between the stubbing out of one cigarette and the lighting up of the next.

Lydia has often wondered if Dr. Tepper was originally a medical student who flunked out. He's the only veterinarian she's ever known who talks about dogs and cats using the iatric "we."

"I assume we're not going into Mexico anymore," he says.

Lydia says no, but she's really not sure. This had been her plan before Ralph got sick, and Dr. Tepper knows about it because she had to ask him for the vaccination records and health certificate so that Ralph could be readmitted to the United States. What she wants to do is to stop in El Paso and take Ralph briefly across the Mexican border. Somehow this is important to her: anything to do with airplanes and international borders and the way faces look when they have been somewhere you haven't. When Lydia was nine years old, before she had ever been in a plane herself, her next door neighbors had a pair of Scotties, and as she stood against the fence listening to the peppery staccato of their barking, she was fascinated to think that little Angus and Kyle had been up in a plane, coming from California. She would look at those dogs for long moments, trying to see if any residue of that flight was still visible in their stern little faces.

Ralph has already been in a plane, and if Lydia manages to get him into Mexico, he will be a truly international cat—the first one she's even known, if you don't count Canada. She can imagine that if he lives long enough it will be fun to show him off to her new acquaintances, the first time she has people over for dinner at her new apartment.

"You know," she will say as he pads from guest to guest beneath the red and brown concentric Navajo yarn constructions that by that time she will have put up on the walls, "he's been to Mexico."

She has another plan too, now that he is so sick, and this one she hasn't told anybody about. As soon as he dies, she has decided, she is going to take him to a furrier and have him made into a hat. Sort of a Davy Crockett style is what she is thinking—that might work well with his light gray stripes—but without the tail; the tail hanging down would be a little gross. If he can't be her cat, she has been telling herself since the day Tepper first announced that "we" had tested positive for Feline Leukemia Virus, then he will have to be her hat.

* * *

Texas thins out the next day into nubbled ridges and faraway gray tablelands. Ralph moans from time to time and stares through the bars of his carrier, moving something around inside his mouth, like an old man gumming the sores on his tongue. It is strange how little she feels for him now. Maybe that's the one merciful thing about FeLV: the personality is the first thing to go. By the time they are about to die, there's nobody to say good-bye to anymore.

She feels clearer in the sinuses already. Unfortunately, the main thing she notices at this point is how bad everything smells: the sweetish vinyl polish inside the truck cab, Ralph's deep yellow urine, a truckload of hogs up ahead, their thick outhouse odor trailing for miles behind them in the traffic.

Strange to think, in a country with MRI systems and CAT scans and little synthetic molecules that can fit into the puzzle pieces of the brain's wiring as cleanly as a digital key fits into the door of a Ramada Inn, that she had to spend five years feeling lousy, in the middle of a city of hospitals, and that after all the shots and pills and vaporizers, the most sophisticated advice her doctor could finally give her was to get out of town.

Everybody at work was wonderful about it. The director of customer relations at Procter and Gamble went out of her way to help Lydia find a good job at the Tucson office of IBM. The whole office held a party for her, gave her a card: "We're all sad you're leaving. Even the computer's down."

One of her friends drew her a cartoon showing the Four Horsemen of the Apocalypse (he labeled them Manny, Moe, Jack, and Shemp) breaking down the door to a deserted office marked 666. Inside the door, Lydia's computer, her phone console, and her desk, with its array of pill bottles and inhalers and nasal sprays, were strung with cobwebs.

The joke in this drawing had to do with Lydia's main function in the customer relations department. She had become the person who had to deal with customer inquiries about the number 666, which some religious groups believed was concealed within the company's trademark.

Lydia's job, as the 666 specialist, was to talk to those callers and explain that it was a hoax, to offer to send them a booklet that included the story of how the venerable trademark actually came to be, and, lately, to explain that P&G was suing two franchisees of a well-known pyramid-scheme cleaning products marketer, who were being charged with maliciously distributing a photocopied handout that accused P&G of being in league with Satan. She was also supposed to put a tracer on anyone who was blatantly threatening, though the tracers led almost always to public telephones.

She was good at it. It was the best feeling of the whole job, even on days when the bones around her nose felt as if she were twenty feet underwater, when she could actually calm down some born-again housewife and get her to admit that she missed being able to use Ivory soap. Sometimes a warm tingle would run up Lydia's neck, almost getting to the place where it would let the pressure out of her sinuses, on those occasions when she heard the voice on the other end soften and say good-bye without anger.

But most of the time it didn't work that way. Somehow 800 numbers always bring out the worst in people. Monday mornings were especially bad, in the lingering flush of Pentecostal gatherings from the day before. Women would ask a question about the Devil and then never stop talking long enough for her to answer.

The problem with talking to that kind of people all day was that later, when she went out into the real world and waited in line at the supermarket, she could never stop wondering who the angry ones were. Everybody always looks so normal and relaxed waiting in traffic; only after they're pulling away do you see the Assembly of God bumper sticker, furious in its red-white-and-blue block lettering. Every time Lydia and the man she had been seeing went to a Reds game together, she found herself paying less attention to the players than to the faces of strangers passing in the stands, wondering which ones God was talking to and which fathers were there not because they liked baseball but because they couldn't think of any other approved family things to do with the children. Some of those fathers had to be up there somewhere, on the other side of the field, hidden in the tweedish, red-sprinkled texture of crowd—sitting, staring, all that anger about the sixes compressed, hidden in their little family hearts like a handgun under a gang member's jacket.

* * *

In the El Paso Comfort Inn East, Ralph lies on his back on Lydia's lap, being force-fed. He seems to be calmly swallowing the molasses-brown amalgam of protein and vitamins and fat that she slowly pushes into his mouth from the graduated cylinder of the oral syringe. Then suddenly the muscles of his mouth and neck move forward in a spasm, and everything pours down the gray fur on the sides of his face, like a clownish extension of his mouth. He didn't swallow any of it. It would ordinarily be funny, but Ralph doesn't have a personality anymore. This is no funnier than paint dripping down a wall.

She wipes off what she can, looks into Ralph's blank eyes, and sees at once that he's not going to make it to Arizona. She does not cry because there is no longer anybody there to cry over, just a sick animal with a big cartoon Mexican mustache of Nutri-Vite running down the sides of his face.

So Ralph almost certainly won't be there when she has her first dinner party, which means that it won't matter by that time if he has ever made it to Mexico or not. But for some reason it seems even more important now than before, in the little time he has left. Plus, she has the papers from Dr. Tepper, and it seems pathetic to get the papers for something and then not do it.

"Mexico." That's what she says. She paces barefoot on the soft pinkish carpet, stepping around where she has set Ralph down and he has returned to his crouch without taking a step, bundled up in more or less the same shape he will be when be becomes a hat, if she can find somebody to do the job.

Ralph's whole life passes before her eyes as she walks around the motel room—all his travels, all the states he's been to; even cats are cosmopolitan these days. Born in Indiana, moved to Ohio, driven to Pennsylvania, New Jersey, Delaware, New York, other states she can't remember, yowling in the same carrier. And once by plane, unescorted, from Boston to Cincinnati, coming in shit-smeared and stinking on the U.S. Airways baggage wagon.

Now she does feel like crying but not enough to really do it. She paces, sniffing the motel's heavy carpet perfume with every inhalation. You would think that in these nonsmoking rooms they would need to use less fragrance instead of more.

And Tucson, everybody talks about how great Tucson is supposed to be: its sunlit avenues lined with cactusy gift shops, its good standing on the musical theater circuit, and its new Hispanic-American-Apache desert cuisine, which has been written up in *Gourmet* magazine, emphasizing green peppers grilled over mesquite.

But Lydia is prepared to face what she really expects to find there—the land of the allergic, the home of the geriatric: widowers in those supposedly glaucoma-preventive praying mantis goggles pushing their grocery wagons, called "buggies" out there, through the aisles of a store where for some reason Hellmann's has been renamed Best Foods mayonnaise.

Outside it will be so bright that if you forget your sunglasses, you will hardly be able to squint long enough to see the saguaros at the edge of the parking lot, poking up through the skin of the earth like something for which the doctor would recommend an immediate biopsy. She knows it's beautiful, but there's something horrible about it too, the unforgiving, Old Testament glare of light. She could see it everywhere last month on her apartment-hunting trip: the sun slamming down all day over all that cataclysmic beauty—if you can call it beauty—where the hills don't seem quite finished, and the valleys look like abandoned bauxite mines.

The manager of her apartment complex has warned her that her car's dashboard will crack in a week if she doesn't get one of those cardboard protectors that everybody puts under their windshields. She has already promised herself that when she gets one, she will never leave it up, the way most people seem to, with the "HELP! CALL POLICE!" side facing out. Decision taken: Ralph is going to Mexico.

* * *

When you get close to the border you can feel it, in the low clutter of cement-block houses, in the sunblasted look of storefronts. She drives the van, with the car following on the towing dolly, down streets full of signs for *Cambianos* posted above bulletproof money-changing windows, each with a concavity under the glass to pass the currency through. She has found a Mexican station on AM. The announcer's voice seems to be charged by some rapid and outlandish voltage, his syllables swooping up to a high note, then swinging down through an electronic reverberation of excitement. She took two years of that language in college and now she can barely make out a word.

Everyone on the pedestrian section of the Stanton Street Bridge walks in the same direction; you get back into the United States on a different bridge. Below, visible through the cross-hatched security bars that run along the side of the walkway, the Rio Grande flows along the bottom of a narrow sluiceway sunk in the center of a white expanse of concrete. She is over the water now, the cat carrier swinging gently at her side, with Ralph's veterinary papers tucked into a compartment, certifying that he is not dying of any disease—and now beyond it, walking downhill toward the barred full-height steel turnstile that lets people into Ciudad Juárez. He is in Mexico.

Lydia stops nowhere, walking beside the traffic of Avenida 16 de Septiembre with her half-alive luggage, toward the other bridge that goes back to the U.S., through the charcoal-sweet restaurant smoke, the oily, distinctively Mexican exhaust, and the soft bubble-gum smell that hangs over every corner. She buys nothing from the wagons of ceramic dogs and fringed miniature sombreros, smiles blankly at the black-haired children who beg for coins and stare into the cat case.

* * *

The next day Ralph can't walk. Lydia props him up and he falls down, breathing hard. Outside the room, kids are shrieking and doing cannonballs. It's one of those motels set up around a sort of atrium, where all three stories of rooms face inward onto the trapped noise of the pool.

She should have planned ahead about the hat. Whether it can be done now on such short notice is problematic; maybe if she just had him skinned she could send the pelt to a hat stylist when she has time—which is a gross thought, but really when you think about it no grosser than putting him in a hole and letting fly larvae eat him. She holds him on her lap and pets him, feeling every bone through the diminished flesh; his head hangs down as if to stare at the floor. On television, Bob Barker announces, with a nectar of love in his voice, that his next contestant on *The Price Is Right* is eighty-five years young.

Lydia wonders what the fur-hating Bob would say if he could see her this morning, with a live animal on her lap, and the motel phone book on the table opened to "Taxi" and "Taxidermy." She can see that there is something cruel about that old man's face, even as he fawns over his contestants, something sharp-toothed, hard, like the faces she used to imagine on the other end of the 666 line, face muscles clenched around the bones of their jaws like a fist.

Actually, Ralph might make a very good hat, now that he is just about finished with being a cat. His dignified gray stripes will go well with the winter gray of the air in a city, perhaps Chicago, sometime when she flies up there in non-allergy season.

* * *

"No ma'am," the first taxidermist says, in the gentle Texas drawl of a man not tough enough to have been a cowboy. "We just do fish 'n game here."

"Sorry," another tells her, "I don't do *pets,*" coming down hard on that last word, as if there is perhaps in this region a whole underground dead pet business that decent family people hate. One more time, in her most diplomatic office voice, putting some warmth into it, the way she did with those toll-free callers who actually sounded as if they could be persuaded away from believing in the Sixes:

"Good morning. I'm on my way through El Paso, and I have a rather unusual request."

"Tell you the truth, ma'am, I don't know anybody in this state who could do that."

* * *

In the pamphlets Lydia used to read when she was waiting with Ralph in Dr. Tepper's waiting room, it always says that the veterinarian will let you stay in the treatment room if you want to be there to witness the putting-to-sleep process. She has always imagined that it must be a very healthy bonding experience for families. But they don't permit that in this clinic. She can't make him into a hat, and now it turns out she can't even watch him die.

It takes a long time. The waiting room has no magazines, no Hartz Mountain pet care pamphlets, nothing to read at all except one of those very poorly organized wall posters showing all the breeds of dogs in the world, in which it's impossible to find which description refers to which drawing. How sick she is of these hard-surfaced waiting rooms, with their piss-and-Lysol smell, now stronger than ever in her clearing nose, their bare floors and their vulcanized vinyl couches, like the seats of a school bus.

Outside, she walks in the sunshine, in a kind of ovenish heat that makes her face and hands tingle but leaves her skin sweatless under the dry warmth of her clothes, toward the red *K* of Kmart, where she would like to find a more comfortable pair of sunglasses. But the spaces out here can play tricks on you. She turns back when she notices that she isn't getting any closer.

* * *

Ralph has come back double-wrapped, one blue plastic bag inside another. The doctor was required by Texas law to clean and disinfect the body. Lydia can feel that the fur is slippery with cleaning fluid. She doesn't say much. The receptionist must think she's some kind of cold fish, to be able to slide her American Express card across the desk as casually as if she's paying for a business lunch, and then to walk out blank-faced, without even having to put her sunglasses on, holding the empty traveling case in one hand, in the other a bag of Ralph, made heavier by the deadness she has just paid fifty dollars for.

By the time she has waited through the first long traffic light between the veterinary clinic and the ramp back on to the interstate, she has already decided that there will be no funeral. To have a funeral you have to pray, and Lydia's standard joke with her friends is that she cannot pray because she is not a Republican. She is thinking, now that Ralph can't be her Chicago hat, that the proper western burial would be to leave him out somewhere in the desert, as dinner for the coyotes. She is pretty sure that feline leukemia cannot be transferred over into latran leukemia. She has always loved coyotes, those beautiful dogs with their sidelong, haunted faces, and their bleached eyes, and the durable scruff of their coats that Price-Is-Right Bob cannot tolerate seeing on a woman's back.

* * *

At a parking area whose sign announces No Facilities, she parks the truck and walks away from the roadway, along a path that curves behind a low rocky hill. The blue package swings at her side. Tufts of toilet paper, white as chicken feathers and half compressed into a sort of poisoned papier-mâché, mark the places around the trail where motorists couldn't wait for the real rest areas. She examines the ground closely as she walks, knowing that only the lucky ones had paper.

She crosses a chain-link fence at the low point where others have tramped over it, walks a hundred yards further, until the footpath has dwindled away and she seems to be out of toilet paper territory. She can't see the interstate. It's rangeland out here:

flat rocks and hardened mud with some kind of leathery-leaved bushes stirring around in the wind. It's hot, in that western way you feel mostly on the bare parts of your skin. Some bloom, or decay, in the desert has filled the air with something Lydia's half-recovered nasal passages have never smelled before: a deep, spicy, scorched odor—something myrraceous and dehydrated, almost electrical, as if ragweed pollen had been sprinkled on overheated car batteries.

She opens the outer bag, then the inner bag, and pulls him out. He's clean and wet, all the force-feeding mess on his face gone, the gray fur draggled into little tufts, like a newborn animal, still warm, still loose in the joints. A strong peppermint smell, from the doctor's disinfectant, overpowers the sagey breeze of the desert.

She sets him on his side on a flat rock. She does not say good-bye. It occurs to her that maybe she *is* a cold fish. But then, you get that way, like a geriatric nurse overseeing the last weeks of what the obituaries always refer to as a "long illness."

What she hopes mostly is that the coyotes will get to him before the vultures and that they will not be put off by Ralph's peppermint smell. Coyotes are not known for being fastidious, but Lydia is too much of an outsider here to make predictions about the behavior of wild animals.

She pulls back out onto the interstate, the motor winding out to its familiar howl. The van, as usual, is almost out of gas. When a cat dies it leaves nothing behind. It is hard to remember anything but the color of its fur. Lydia has noticed that home videos taken of her friends' animals, even if they are played back just a few weeks after death, give a peculiarly unconvincing, cartoonish quality to things like the jerky motion of a cat's tail as it runs up the front steps of a house.

Perhaps it's an illusion, or exhaustion, or the thin air, or some neurological side effect of the pressure in her sinuses letting off, but when she opens the window, to air out the residual peppermint, she seems to catch a whiff, even through the heat, of Labor Day weekend in the high desert, the coolish breeze of work and school starting up again, the days counting down to the beginning of September with the same regularity as the green mileposts that count down through the single digits toward the "Welcome to Arizona" billboard that Lydia can make out, still a few miles in the distance.

Whether this move is a mistake or not she doesn't know (already having a thought entirely removed from Ralph, she notices), whether the men in the offices next to hers will be there by choice or by allergist's orders remains to be seen. She counts it as a good sign, though, as the van-and-car combination clumps over the seam in the pavement between states, that the governor of Arizona watches over the incoming traffic with the kind of confident smile that shows him to be the kind of person who would never have to move away from home because of something going wrong with his nose.

hungry hungry hippos

In my first year out of college, I spent so much time staring into my old black-and-white television that I began to incorporate into my own eyes the tendency of the picture to roll when the tubes overheated. Drifting off to sleep, I often had vertical-hold problems: the hypnagogic images would travel upward, slowly, framed by dark bands above and below. I remember waking up angry during those days, then starting to laugh, quilted under three blankets and the comforter of a zipped-open sleeping bag in my half of a winterized bungalow, its forced-air vents cut into the ceiling where the warm air stayed and stayed.

It was the seventies, and it was gloomy, of course. For those of us who had graduated from Sugarloaf College the year after it lost its accreditation, things were so bleak that we boasted in our letters to one another how badly we were doing. I was living in my first nonstudent apartment, in the middle of what had once been a Jewish summer resort, a cluster of reconditioned cabins amid rows of abandoned ones trailing off into the woods. When my summer landscaping had ended and I applied for unemployment benefits, I was amazed by how little pressure was put on me to find a job; nobody said a word when I listed my desired occupation as "shepherd."

But even in those days things were happening, although nobody who watched a lot of discussion shows could have believed it. Properties were passing from owner to owner with a firm handshake; new buildings were going up in which prosperous things would someday happen. In the interim between the closing down of some place and its resurrection into the mainstream of wealth, there may develop for a few years an easygoing slum life—clunky old oversized cars roaring out of driveways, black-and-white televisions casting a flat light among armchairs with white stuffing bulging through the holes that dogs have chewed. There grew, into the blank space of this tract waiting to be rezoned and bulldozed away for offices, a brambly tenement presence, with domestic disputes, people whose telephones had been disconnected asking me to call the police on each other, cars having to be jump-started—including one car that had been hooked to another with jumper cables and whose battery exploded with the force of a cherry bomb.

There was a nervous slum comfort every afternoon, with the snow blowing outside the curtainless windows and the furnace going on and off, as I sat for hours in front of *Magilla Gorilla* and *Bewitched* and *Hollywood Squares*. I could put off for another day collecting whatever new insufficient funds notice waited in a small envelope braced diagonally in the post office box that I had rented because the snowplows kept knocking the regular boxes down. I would navigate through the day's *TV Guide* listings, staying away from anything too close to those days, ignoring the slow-moving soaps with their hair-sprayed construction workers out of jobs, avoiding the prime-time sitcoms with the precocious child star chirping out shrill jokes about the gas shortage. Every time somebody won the grand prize on *The $20,000 Pyramid*, I would get up out of my seat and jump up and down a few times in front of the set, just like the winning contestants. The floor of the bungalow creaked beneath my feet, and the motion of my weight jogged the picture tube into its own celebratory series of flips.

I noticed that in commercials for children's games—even though we had been taught at Sugarloaf that kids did not really want to be competitive—it was still essential that the winner say, "*I win!*" The advertisers must have done some elaborate psychological testing, and it must have worked, because Hungry Hungry Hippos had stayed on the market for over ten years. The object of the game is to press your handle down again and again as fast as you can, with no timing, no strategy, just slam-slam-slam as your hippo surges out to grab marble after marble from the game surface encircled by other players aged four to twelve, one of whom will soon shout, "*I win!*"

My favorite commercial was for the lightbulb-powered Pizza Hut Baking Oven, in which you could make a wafer-size pie from the accompanying crust and topping mixes. The tape for that commercial had a skip in it, which they never fixed, half a beat somehow spliced out of the song's rhythm. To a bouncy tarantella, with accordions, the children's voices sang, "Pizza Hut, Pizza Hut / Just wait until you try / The pizza that you make yourself . . ." and here half a second had been cut away from the pause between phrases, so that they ran together as "The pizza that you make your SELFA tasty pizza pie!" That was the moment I loved most: sitting in front of the set and singing along precisely with the gap in the tape, laughing at how broken everything was—the couch half-collapsed, the windowpanes rattling in the percussion of somebody's bad muffler outside, the dishes in my Rubbermaid drainer rattling whenever I walked across the carpeted plywood floor.

* * *

There is a peculiar hazy blue that flickers from a black-and-white set on a winter afternoon when you are walking outside and look through a window into the darkness of somebody else's living room. There is a leisurely, tidal rhythm to which defective television screens used to roll, which perhaps a new generation of transistors no longer permits.

The sky in those days—blank as the periods of dead air between television shows and hanging over my head like an hour with nothing to watch—seemed so solid, so permanent, that it was hard to imagine my bungalow neighborhood as it had existed in the fifties and sixties, as a summer place for people who couldn't afford the fancy resorts like Grossinger's.

It would have been lush and green in those days, with bushes trimmed back from the paths where I sometimes walked when I needed to let whatever was overheated inside my television cool down. The summer evening would be full of dinner smells: hamburger patties dripping fat onto the hot briquettes in those old stand-up cookers, barbecue sauce burning, the sweet garlic smell of Hebrew National hot dogs, and the mild petroleum vapor of charcoal lighter fluid. And there would be the usual neighborhood sounds, softened by the absorbent foliage: the piercing notes of children, parents shouting from house to house through the screened windows, radios and televisions ringing through the forest late into the daylight hours of a summer night still bright at seven-thirty.

It was strange to walk among the abandoned buildings and think what the lives inside them must have been like, in a resort too humble to have a tennis court or a tummler: weekly budgets written out on yellow paper, serious discussions about the future, cash doled out into a series of labeled envelopes. And it was hard to imagine what those people would have thought about what replaced them: a life that draped itself with a strange, erotic slovenliness over the swaybacked couches, everywhere the over-flowing ashtrays and past-due MasterCharge statements, dishes piled in the sink for days, and outside the window always the same white, featureless sky.

* * *

I would like to think that certain unrelated places and times can possess one shade of light in common. There is a particular tone of light I first noticed during my Sophomore Trimester Abroad, when my friends and I took a side trip from London up to Liverpool. I remember how solidly the cloud cover hung over us as we stared at the Liverpool Anglican Cathedral. Huge and gloomy, it stood on the high ground of a rock outcropping, across from where my *Beatles History Guidebook* had directed us to John Lennon's former apartment.

Even now I like to imagine John Lennon, in the late fifties, his hair greased back, walking out the door of 3 Gambier Terrace every day in the same overcast light, looking across to that ty-rannical structure. The early songs, like "There's a Place" and "It Won't Be Long," would be taking shape in his mind, high, thin sounds with harmonicas, while the cathedral just stood there sulking, massive, waiting to be redeemed by the sharp-edged tone of a Rickenbacker electric twelve-string.

During the noisy weeks of that British trimester, I could not have imagined the silence my classmates and I would soon be graduating into. I could not have foreseen how important the cartoons and commercials on my little Zenith portable would become, ringing through so many long afternoons, with songs for Cocoa Puffs and Malibu Barbie's Beach Bus. In the months after graduation, everything seemed wounded. The toy tanks and troop carriers advertised on television had been demobilized into Wilderness Adventure Wagons. G.I. Joe was now disarmed, bearded, sensitive.

It was horrible just to glance at the newspapers that cluttered my bungalow when I was checking the classifieds every day. Even music had been wounded, sculpted and styled into the artsy rococo of Yes and Genesis. The only program produced in those days that I can still bring myself to care about is the old *Mary Tyler Moore Show*, especially the shots of Mary walking through Minneapolis on a winter day or hurrying across the street with a bag of groceries in her arms.

* * *

I am sitting here in the nineties thinking about days in the seventies when I chose to live and walk among the remains of the fifties and sixties and could have used some encouragement about the eighties. I would like to go back and tell myself that the low overcast I remember having always been up there had a remarkable amount of space above it, that it was really not the sky at all, only a kind of drop ceiling—as in the joke Italians would soon be telling about the new pope's plan to remodel the Sistine Chapel.

It would have been enough if I could have known only that the sun was there above the bungalows, that after a few years my poverty would prove to be as insubstantial as my education, and that there would be a moment in the future—I would be on business, with somebody else paying for it—when my plane would break through the top of the clouds. It will be the first time in days that I have seen the open sky. The plane's shadow shrinks downward, ringed by a dull rainbow, until the clouds flatten out into a yeasty froth like the surface of brewery wort.

All over the cabin on a morning flight you can smell the coffee as it is rolled down the narrow aisle on its stainless steel wagon. The same in-flight magazine peeks from every seat pocket. Those who didn't bring newspapers with them will soon be "Discovering the Secrets of San Diego."

You can tell that it's winter by the smallness of the sun as it slants into the rounded windows on the other side of the aircraft—a row of them, like television sets in an appliance store. You can look down into the cloud cover, paced off by the trailing edge of the wing, and think of all the towns hidden under it, all the real estate in various stages of transition from residential zoning to temporary slum to commercial frontage.

I particularly like to think about Minneapolis, about how it looks in color, these days, in the opening credits of Mary's show—an aerial view of downtown, everything in the low skyline tinted a deep red. A smiling, frightened Mary Tyler Moore steers her white Mustang onto the downtown exit ramp of her new city. The colors in the tape my local station uses are so distorted that when Mary smiles, with the sun through the windshield lighting her face, she looks as if she has gold teeth.

I love to watch her as she drives into the rusty shades of a city that lives from decade to decade in a perpetual winter of jagged chimneys, plumes of rising steam, and that pointed brown clock tower in the middle of downtown. People in long overcoats are hurrying in and out of elevators, rushing along the overhead walkways, which in the winter are the only way to get anywhere. Old green-and-white municipal buses pass by. Mary stops in the middle of the sidewalk, bundled against the cold in a navy blue coat with silver buttons, and like a discus thrower winding up, or like a kid in the commercial for the Super Zoomerang, she spins around in a slow-motion twirling of freeze-frames and throws her hat up into the air.

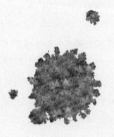

burt osborne
rules the world

All day long, on that day in the sixth grade when my life changed forever and the world became a better place, everything had been smelling and tasting like overcooked eggs. I wasn't sick exactly; it was more that I was no longer friends with the taste of food. Through the last abbreviated class periods and the final rehearsals for the annual St. Vitus Academy Christmas pageant, I smelled eggs everywhere, hard and cheesy on people's breath, tasted them in the green-sprinkled Christmas tree cookies they gave us, in the red lipstick that Mrs. Carmody put on everybody's mouth. Outside, the darkness lay flat against the windows, which I had never before looked out of at night; indoors, everything seemed soaked in yellow dye.

The egg smell grew stronger. I could smell it in the not very clean fabric of my three kings burnoose with the construction-paper crown fitted over the hood. The air on the stage was thick with the smell as we stood waiting for the curtain to open; when it did, the lights were so bright that we could not see the slanted audience from which handclapping cascaded like the sound of water down a wide rapid.

And it came to pass that Jimmy Taurozzi and Ursula Byatt walked from inn to cardboard inn under multicolored floodlights that threw everybody's shadow in three directions, with little overlapping rainbows around the edges. How slowly the Holy Family moved, Jimmy with his long shepherd's crook in one hand, his other arm around Ursula. Even the innkeepers, shaking their heads to say "No room," seemed to be moving like dolls with weak batteries. I could feel pressure building under my chin where my hood had been fastened around my face with a safety pin.

By the time the Christ child had been wrapped in swaddling clothes and placed on Mary's lap, reclining so that His eyes closed by a gravity mechanism, I was feeling distinctly ill. Patrick Dizzini read from St. Luke. Danny McDade, as Melchior, recited "Shiny gold, the gift I bring / To honor Jesus, newborn King," knelt, and laid his box before the manger. I felt a flush of sweat on my forehead; all the hair follicles of my legs were tingling. Keith Wheeler, the only black boy in St. Vitus, spoke Balthazar's line: "Frankincense is mine to give, / That we may all through Jesus live."

And then the spotlight shifted onto me and my myrrh. I could feel something pressing into the soft tissue beneath my chin. Then slowly, as if some higher power were controlling my body, I felt myself bending forward— and in a long arc that sparkled in the multicolored stage lights, I was sick.

What I remember most is the sound from the audience, the simultaneous gasp of two hundred pairs of lungs inhaling. For five seconds nobody moved; then Ursula Byatt, who smelled it, tossed the Christ child into the manger and ran off the stage holding her hand over her mouth. Over the rising murmur of the audience, Mrs. Carmody whisked the curtains shut so fast that the bottoms trailed behind in the air.

I was led backstage, where I sat on a folding metal chair and threw up some more into an empty steam tray that somebody had brought from the cafeteria. As Mrs. Carmody wiped the vomit and lipstick off my mouth with a Kleenex from her purse, I heard Father Hardy's foghorn voice over the PA system: "We're sorry for the unfortunate delay, ladies and gentlemen, and I trust that our young Magus will be feeling better soon."

* * *

When school started again in January, I was famous. When I walked in the halls of that old school, I could feel people's eyes on me. "Hey, King Vomit!" guys would shout at me on the playground or out the windows if no teacher was in the room. "Hey Barf-thazar!"

Another kid made up a song, and he sang it well into January: "We three kings of Orient 'ore': / Bearing gifts, we puke on the floor."

What I soon realized was that I loved it: the hush when I walked into a room where people had been talking about me, the low buzz of kids whispering between classes as they went the other way in the monitored traffic: "That's the guy who threw up in the Christmas pageant."

But by February I was just a normal kid again, which I'd always been and which had never bothered me, but now it hurt. I used to lie awake nights with the window open a crack, listening to the Connecticut Turnpike with its long shapeless hush and thinking of the way the audience gasped that night, how silent the room was for the seconds that their mouths hung open. When you think about all those people out there in the cars on the Turnpike, all the places they're going; when you think how nobody will ever be surprised by anything that ever happens, from the moment their cars are brand-new until the time their cars end up in the same junkyard that their previous car ended up in; when you think about such things, or at least when I thought about them, I realized that I was going to have to do something about it.

* * *

Life is strict. To be a kid in Connecticut, at least in our part of it, is to live in a world protected against anything you could imagine doing to make it more interesting. It is a state without firecrackers, without condom dispensing machines, a state where for some obscure tax reason even the mail-order practical jokes that the Johnson-Smith company advertises in the inside back cover of comic books may not be shipped.

So many contests and free merchandise offers were "Void in Connecticut" that it was all I could do to think up a few jokes within the family at least, while the outside world went on as usual. I used to help my sister Kathy with her homework, and sometimes when she wasn't looking, I would insert the word *fuck* into one of her answers. Or I would slip a raw egg, wrapped in wax paper with a twist of salt, into her lunch box.

It didn't matter that I never got to see the results of any of these tricks; just to know that somewhere out of my sight and hearing, a teacher's mouth was dropping open or at a lunch table Kathy was trying to mop up the egg mess while her friends laughed—just to know those things made me walk through the day with a sort of buzz at the end of my fingers, like the feeling of having an important letter in the mail. And at the end of the day, when Kathy would come home with her face blotched with tears, I was happy, not because I didn't like her, but because it was her job, in the absence of anybody more important, to be the carrier of my jokes into the world.

In the spring, I discovered that it did not hurt to put a grass-hopper into my mouth. At recess I could go up to Mary Ann Blossom or Julie Conklin, saying, "Help me, I think my tooth is broken!" and she would come close to look, and as I opened my mouth, the grasshopper would jump out at her face. When I did this, girls would shriek as if in a horror movie, so loudly that all the other noise on the playground would stop.

"It's Burt Osborne," everybody would say.

I never wanted to hurt anybody. But I knew I couldn't avoid it. The days of the week kept marching single file in school uniforms even duller than the ones we were forced to wear. The Turnpike traffic kept rushing all night like something that doesn't know if it's dead or just asleep. I wrote a fake letter to Kathy's pen pal in Scotland, saying that we all hated her guts. At the dinner table I passed Kathy the almost-empty milk pitcher, pretending to strain with the weight, and when she took it from my hand, ready for it to be full, she involuntarily jerked it upward, and the milk flew out, most of it landing on my mother's plate.

At school the grasshopper situation got so bad that girls refused to go outside after lunch. Other boys had picked up the habit of putting grasshoppers in their mouths. Father Hardy finally had to make an announcement in front of the school assembly.

"We have a new rule, effective immediately …." He spoke from deep within his bronchial tubes, drawing out the syllables of each word into long, tremulous musical notes—the same quality of voice that he would become locally famous for years later. He would even get on *CBS News* once, for conducting public "Death

Masses," in which God was implored to strike down Sen. Lowell Weicker:

"There will be *nooooooo* catching ..." he said, "of *grasshoppers*."

* * *

Some things in my family we weren't supposed to talk about. We weren't supposed to talk about whose fault it was that my father had an ulcer. We weren't supposed to talk about why I was switched to public school after the sixth grade, although my parents often mentioned that the high school system had a better reputation than the elementary. Sometimes at the dinner table, I stared and stared at the window, listening to everybody else talk and knowing that anything I could imagine saying would rub somebody the wrong way.

On Valentine's Day of my first year in Avon Junior High, the choral music teacher had us stand in a circle to play a game in which each student had to think of the title of a song with the word *love* in it. When our turn came, we each had to *sing* the song's title; the first person to fail to come up with a legitimate song would be out of the game.

The music class was a big group, three regular classes crammed into one room. I was halfway around the circle from where we began, from "Why Must I Be a Teenager in Love?" to "Love Is a Many-Splendored Thing" through dozens of songs. From "Will You Love Me Tomorrow?" to "Why Do Fools Fall in Love?" I could see that soon it was going to be my turn.

I could feel my mouth going dry, could feel the burden weighing down on me. I knew I had no choice but to be Burt Osborne, to take that roomful of people and give them something to remember all day long, as I had to take control of every room I walked into, must let my reputation become a giant bodyguard escorting me down every lunch-smelling corridor.

I took a deep breath, the blank faces of the choral music class all around me. And then in a spastic tuneless melody of very high notes and very low notes, I sang out to the three combined classes:

"I *love* to eat *rotten eggs*!"

I want to tell you that the laughter from that class burst into the air with such plosive force that it would not have been a surprise to me if windows had broken. My ears rang. Girls were turning red, not so much from embarrassment as from the sheer pulmonary exertion of laughing at Burt Osborne. The class laughed so loudly that, as Mrs. Winikoff led me down the hall to the principal's office, teachers and students crowded the doors of neighboring classrooms, wondering what had happened. All the way down the hall, I could hear that room ringing with laughter, until we turned a corner and the sound was lost.

The next day I was sent to the school psychologist, who asked me what town we were in and who the president of the United States was, and told me to draw a picture of a person, any person I chose. I drew a picture of a man with the top of his head removed just above the eyebrows and a city of skyscrapers growing from the flat surface where his brains would have been. The detached dome of his head floated above, and from that dome, held by strings like the sheet lines of a parachute, hung a tiny bicycle. When the psychologist asked me about the person, I told him that the man's name was Dr. Keroojalolly and that he had taught me how to rob banks. The psychologist looked at me, earnest, well-meaning, baffled, drained, his eyes empty, his head tilted like a dog's with the effort of understanding, as the lights in the little office reflected off the shiny skin where his black hair was receding. It was wonderful to think I could have such power over someone so much bigger than me. I told him that my parents drank out of the toilet. I said my house was patrolled by flying potatoes.

* * *

I never wanted to hurt anybody. At least I never wanted to hurt them badly. When my father went into Good Samaritan because his ulcer had become perforated (because of me, it was understood without saying), it seemed appropriate somehow that the rules of the hospital would prohibit me from seeing him. During visiting hours Kathy and I waited at home with all the lights on, not saying much, eating Swanson fried chicken dinners, then wandering around the house. Kathy was crying. She didn't understand the difference between an ulcer and cancer, so she thought he was going to die. I would have liked to put my arm around her and tell her everything was all right, but I knew she didn't trust me. I wanted to tell her that I was sorry about all the raw eggs, but I knew I would do it again, someday when Dad was better.

When I say I never wanted to hurt anybody, I say it with the full understanding that I have hurt every person in my family and most of my friends. But you have to understand what it's like to live within earshot of the Connecticut Turnpike: so many nights with all that untouchable machinery going by, so many Mondays when I hadn't done my homework. The way the dead air of schools hung over everything like sheets draped over the furniture in an abandoned house; the way summer plods into fall and never into anything else, and all the stores run back-to-school sales; the way airplanes seem to take hours to come out the other end of a cloud; the way towns go on and on all night and never turn into amusement parks; the way people drive so carefully that you can stand for days at the busiest intersection in town without seeing a single accident—all these horrible, dead, dusty, inert *facts* together droned on forever all night, until I couldn't stand it. Sometimes I could imagine that they had joined together to become the voice of the Connecticut Turnpike telling me that I was on this earth to make it the kind of place that people would remember having lived on even after they were dead.

Think of all the people who don't know what to do about you, the traffic seemed to be whispering to me (though I know that I was making up the words myself). *Remember where you are: The bottom of the world, Stratford, city of people who drive very carefully, who slow down on bridges because the sign says the bridge freezes before the road. They are not even cowards. To be a coward you have to be a coward about something. These people are less than cowards. They are* timid!

* * *

My father got better. Elizabeth in Scotland stopped answering Kathy's pen pal letters. Mom no longer covered the meat loaf and the spaghetti with her special tomato sauce that I had always loved; by doctor's orders a bland white sauce replaced it.

Spring came, and soon it was time for the annual Avon Junior High spring concert. The seventh grade class was giving a choral reading of a poem called "The First Springtime" by Mary Matthews Cheney. We rehearsed for weeks, practicing how we would alternate between group lines and individual lines.

My solo line was: "And the *moon* shone down on the water!" Mrs. McManus, the chorus director, had instructed me to draw out the word *moon* as long as I could, with my round mouth imitating the shape of the full moon, so that coming after Kim Prozeller's line—"And the Lord held the wind in His fingers,"—my voice would ring out: "And the *moooooooooon* shone down on the water!"

It was the middle of the night when I realized what Burt Osborne had to do, and I sat up straight in my bed, the low breath of the Turnpike droning outside the open window. It was not a decision. It was not anything I had to debate with myself about. It came upon me suddenly, irrevocably, like the moment in the poem we were reciting, when God says, "Let the warm sun shine," and the custodian turns all the spotlights on.

Not that I wasn't scared. The thought of it made my mouth go dry, especially in rehearsal, when I thought about the power I had, the power over those empty seats we rehearsed in front of and practiced projecting at. Every time I spoke my given line about the moon, I could feel a cold chill run through my scrotum, something icy and off balance, the same acrophobic thrill I get if I think about jumping off a cliff.

There we were at last, the slanted seats full of people, the last Parents' Night before the end of school. The auditorium hummed with low voices and rumbled with the lowering of hinged seat bottoms. We stood on three riser levels.

> When God invented springtime,
> He looked around at the bare, gray ground,
> At the white branches, and the black branches,
> And a few birds high in a cold sky.

Our voices were an airy hush of poetry: the first voices of the frogs, the sprouting crocuses, the gathering green. I could feel the vulnerable little audience like a trapped bird. I was just as afraid for them as I was for me. God sat upon His throne. Burt Osborne stood trembling on his riser, knowing that nobody in this whole gathered assembly would ever forget this moment.

My cue was coming. There it was: Kim Prozeller's clear, meticulous, almost prissy voice:

"And the Lord held the wind in His fingers," she said.

I drew in my breath and changed the world.

"And there was a big piece of SHIT hanging out of His ass!"

The sound that rose from the audience in the seconds following the delivery of that line was more than just the sound of three hundred mouths suddenly inhaling. I could *feel* them gasp, could feel the whole auditorium go suddenly short of oxygen.

Everything stopped. We just stood there. Everybody in the world was staring at me with their mouths hanging open, their faces drained and empty, as if the roof above them had blown off and there was nothing at all up there. The seconds went by, the whole world stuck, pinned under the thumb of Burt Osborne.

It was such an important moment in the history of making the world a more interesting place that I would like to construct a time diagram of it, like the diagrams of the first nanoseconds after a nuclear explosion that the left used to post on university bulletin boards.

1 second after line is spoken:

Absolute silence. The echo of the words is absorbed by the soft cloth of everybody's fathers' sport coats.

2 seconds:

A collective intake of breath with a high wheezing overtone, as if they had all sat down on a block of ice.

5 seconds:

Silence again. Everything hangs there. Smithsonian Institution vaporized. The other kids in the chorus don't know if they should keep going.

10 seconds:

They don't keep going. Shifting from foot to foot on the risers, they look for direction from Mrs. McManus, who is already beginning to cry. The murmur starts up in the audience. "Did you *hear* what he *said*?" Some of the girls cry, some of the boys laugh. The curtain closes.

* * *

The ride home in the car that night took place in the most profound silence of all the silent treatments in the life of our family. Kathy sat up front with our parents. Wind whistled through the half-open windows of the car, the way it whistles through the halls of an abandoned house.

Alone in the backseat I felt weightless, as if all the responsibility of being Burt Osborne had been lifted from me. The side of my face burned and tingled where Mrs. McManus had slapped me. Technically that's illegal in a public school, but I could hardly blame her.

All I could do now was sit back and surrender myself to the long progression of punishments to come: the summer school, the grounding, the sequestered meals, the canceled allowance, the psychiatric appointments.

I wish I could say that I feel worse about the trouble I caused: my father's ulcer, Mrs. Carmody's quitting her job, the lost pen pal. But really what I regret more than any of those things is that this night was the most remarkable I would ever let things get. What I'm sorriest about is that I didn't keep going, that I left so many jokes to dry up and die without ever having been played on somebody. It's horrible, at this late date, to think that I never put glue in anybody's hat or lined anybody's shoes with flypaper. In college, my friends and I did all the standard things, of course: broke a few windows, made death threat phone calls to the ROTC program director's wife. Once when a visiting speaker from CCNY came to give a lecture on Dadaism, we were all set to go in there and throw potato salad at him, but my friends got cold feet. And even if we'd done it, it wouldn't have been as much fun; nobody's mouth would have dropped open.

What I'm saying is that I could have done a better job of being Burt Osborne. There was a period of two days in college when I'm reasonably sure I could have made my roommate's girlfriend believe I was a werewolf. She was ready for it, and I didn't do anything. I hate to think about this. Or in drama club when I got to play the part of Hamlet, I could have changed it around, had him kill Claudius in the first act, no more procrastination.

We drove through the spring evening. Street after street passed in silence. In the light through the windshield, I could see the dark shapes of my mother's head and my father's head, with Kathy's smaller head down low in the seat between them. They all seemed to lean close together, so that sometimes, in silhouette, it looked as if the heads of my mother and father had become attached to Kathy's head and had turned into a pair of giant Mickey Mouse ears.

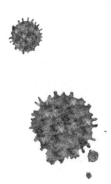

how to swallow

Frank Sinatra was dead, to begin with, but that wasn't the lead story. Cars were on fire in Indonesia, burning yellow and orange on the front page of the same newspaper in every vending box, which Jim could see every time the chartered bus stopped at a corner, the whole page bright with flames, leaving a narrow column on the right: THE VOICE FALLS SILENT.

Around him, the sustaining members of the National Woodwind Association sat calmly in their fragrances. Most of these people were retired music teachers, which made it strange to think that for the whole ride down here, from the convention hotel in Michigan to Elkhart, Indiana, nobody had said a word

about Frank Sinatra, just carried on a mild chatter of grandchildren and weather, all this in a blend of smells that Jim had been
breathing for years on similar contest-judging trips. It was not
unpleasant exactly, just insistent and territorial, making the long
rectangular space of the bus a moving chamber of sweet powders
and aftershaves, so strong cumulatively that Jim imagined he could
smell the confusion of their diverse floral and aldehydic notes not
only when he inhaled, but even when he exhaled, if that was possible, the molecules seeming to bond to his upper nasal tissues.

"So this is what it comes to," Jim said to himself, though he
didn't have any more reason to think it on this trip than on any
of the others. "Riding on the bus with retired people." Actually
he enjoyed coming to these contests and getting paid to wear
his name tag with the word *Judge* on it. He liked how quiet
his house was when he left early in the morning, with classes
cancelled and a note and a check for the cleaning lady taped to
the door, how within a few hours he would be walking around
the campuses of schools better than his own, where for some
reason the men always looked stronger and the women prettier,
everybody standing better, as if their large backpacks weighed
nothing. At these schools even the political announcements, on
sheets of bright goldenrod or acid green paper taped to the base
of lightposts, seemed to have more firepower, almost the same
fury as from his own time in school: END RACIST AGGRESSION
and STOP THE LIES ABOUT THE SENDERO LUMINOSO. The
flyers were illustrated with well-done drawings of clean-faced
young men and women marching forward in a tight pack,
their fists in the air and the sleeves of their work shirts rolled
up, some of their faces shaded with diagonal lines to show
that they are black, others with fewer lines, to represent brown
populations, and all with the same cleanly and cheerfully angry
expression and the same slightly Asiatic cast to their features.

"So this is what it comes to," he said to himself and only to himself, because he knew it was stupid. "Riding on the bus to interesting places."

He had to admit that the Selmer musical instrument plant they had toured actually was an interesting place, especially the guy working the clarinet lathe. Now, before they headed back to the hotel and tonight's final awards banquet, where Jim would stand up and announce the twenty-five thousand dollar winner, they were on their way to an authentic 1890s lunch at the Branch Creek Historical Homestead and Craft Center, which also promised to be interesting because it would include only recipes and ingredients that had been in use at that time.

Kurt VanSickle, one of the directors of the woodwind association and the one who had first invited him out here, sat in the aisle seat next to Jim. He was talking about how he used to prime his students at the University of Dayton for competitions like this.

"I tell them they're playing for their worst enemy," Kurt said, his eyes clear blue under a steel gray crew cut in which the forward-most hair had been left slightly longer than the rest and propped up with wax, nothing like the kind of streamlined buzz cuts you saw on kids these days.

"How so?" Jim said.

"You're up there playing the clarinet—what do you think they want?" Kurt VanSickle was at least seventy, but his face, especially his chin, had a firmness, as if the expression on his face had never relaxed enough for the flesh to droop. He was a broad-shouldered man, about Jim's size, and Jim noticed that the two of them had more of their hair left than any other males on the bus, including the driver.

In the aisle seat on the other side of Kurt, Gwen Stockland, the contest coordinator, leaned over to hear. Like most of the coordinators he had worked with, she was slim and well maintained, about Jim's age, with one of those faces you can talk to for an hour and you know she's still listening.

Kurt went on. "I'm sure you've done enough Shostakovich with Wichita to know what it feels like to hit a squawker. That's what the judges want. The whole thing's *adversarial*."

On that last accented word, Kurt VanSickle turned his face away from Jim toward the bus's windshield, showing his still-strong profile for emphasis, the magnification of his glasses catching the light at a bright angle. He had done the same thing last night in his keynote address every time he made an important point, pausing dramatically and glaring off into a corner of the partitioned assembly room.

When Jim looked up ahead through the windshield, he could see the lead bus where the clarinet contestants were riding. It would have been just as easy to put him up there with the students, but it was flattering to know that Kurt and Gwen wanted to talk to somebody who was still performing in a real woodwind section, which of course was the main reason he kept getting invited to these judgings in the first place, not so much for being chair of a college music department but because of those magical words: *Wichita Symphony Orchestra*. And then it was also possible that Gwen figured since he was nearly fifty, he would be more comfortable surrounded by people closer to his own age.

Maybe she was right. Whatever you do, it's going to close in, and soon you're going to be surrounded by people closer to your own age whether it makes you comfortable or not. Last week, visiting at his parents' condo in Florida, Jim went out running on the beach, but it was too cold, so he walked back briskly across the huge parking lot. As he walked, he saw on all sides other figures, small, in bright pastel sweats, elbows raised cheerfully, walking briskly around the parking lot on their daily constitutionals.

Walking briskly around the parking lot! So this is what it comes to. Then while he was getting ready for the trip out here, he found himself coming out of Wal-Mart in possession of a super jumbo economy size bottle of house brand ibuprofen. By the time he realized what he had purchased, it was too late.

He began to ask himself questions, as if picking at a sore. What kind of people would buy this container? It was almost the size of a bottle of red wine, with the bold letters of the EQUATE brand name specially enlarged, perhaps as a convenience for the visually impaired.

Who would have bought this? Cool teenagers with fake IDs? Cool college students with silver studs through their tongues? (You don't see that with woodwind players, understandably.) Who else? Couples moving into up-and-coming neighborhoods from which poor people have been evicted? Accountants for firms so hip they wear turtlenecks to work and get paid three times as much because they keep three sets of books for each corporation?

Jim knew, sitting there in his car in the Wal-Mart parking lot, that he was asking himself an empty rhetorical question. Only one population existed that would take the time to seek out such a bargain on the long health and beauty shelves and then sit back in the bus, their pain under control, looking out the window at the newspaper vending boxes, the same front page passing again and again, the yellows and oranges of burning cars bright behind the grid of green-painted theft-prevention bars.

"We had two national semifinalists at Dayton when I was chair," Kurt said, showing his profile again. "And let me tell you, I put the killer instinct into those kids."

Jim had been here for a day and a half, and he hardly even knew what the contestants looked like. He had met them only long enough to shake hands, after Kurt's keynote address the first night. At the recitals yesterday, he didn't get to see them at all. By association rule the performances had to take place behind a curtain, on the theory that it was better not to have the judge influenced by extraneous things like pretty girls or pimply high school band types who hold their instruments straight down against their chests or by the way some players have learned to swing their instruments around Pied Piper style, an old clarinet contest trick.

Even through the curtain, though, in a hotel conference room that with the partition pulled closed is called the Saginaw Room and with the partition folded up into its little square closet becomes part of the Grand Rapids Room, you can learn a lot about these kids, their personalities, even their problems, if you listen right. There are the creeps and the charmers, the shy genius, the egotist, the sentimentalist with a little too much vibrato—and then once in a while someone who wants it so badly that he or she knows how to talk to you through the instrument. All Jim knew was that Number 17 had something.

By the timbre of inhaled breaths he could tell it was probably a female student, and he could hear that she was slapping the keys open a little harder than you're supposed to, making a percussion that was audible even on what, from the tone of it, was almost certainly a Peter Eaton.

But there she was, curtain or not, slamming the keys as if she knew he might deduct points but knew they needed to be slammed if she was going to get to the heart of the piece, zigzagging through that Scriabin transcription that she must have been warned some people don't like, talking to Jim, taking him by the arm, musically speaking, the opposite of Kurt VanSickle's killer instinct, telling Jim through the curtain that even if he wasn't big on Scriabin, she was. Then she showed him why, letting the tone tighten in the quiet passages, as if she had squeezed the bore of the instrument smaller, the sound harsh but far away, almost angry, and most of all, *there*, as if she'd cut a hole in the curtain and looked him right in the eyes.

Whatever it was, she had it. Clarinets don't get taken seriously, sometimes not even by the people who play them—or by the people who orchestrate music for them. Real clarinet music is not just about that mellow hollow-bore tone that gets so many elementary school kids attracted to the instrument, and it's not just about the jaunty lines of the *Tancredi* overture or the low-register tiptoe theme of the cat in Prokofiev's *Peter and the Wolf*. A clarinet can have some nastiness in it: the snarling comedy of Klezmer or that weird cadenza in the Borodin concerto, which still scared Jim when he had to play it with the Wichita Symphony Orchestra, because it seemed to be written so that the inevitable mistakes that even a good player makes are going to squeak out like a kid playing an old tin Selmer.

* * *

At the Branch Creek Historical Homestead, strapping young women in bulky old-time dresses, their hair pinned and gathered at the backs of their heads in stiff white bonnets, hurried around with tin milk pitchers.

"Hey, Dr. Garrett!" one of the contestants called, a red-cheeked overweight boy, probably the Gershwin, but you never know. "Sit here, why don't you?"

He hesitated, standing awkwardly and looking around, at a section of the long table with five of the students.

"You've already picked the winner, right?" the kid said. "So you don't have to worry if you picked somebody who turns out to be obnoxious. You don't know us, and we don't know you," he said, grandly. "Right?"

Jim put on a W. C. Fields voice: "Yeah. Let's keep it that way," and they smiled but did not laugh, because of course they did not recognize the voice.

Today's newspaper was spread out on the table. It was strange, and maybe a good sign, to think that these kids, who would have been toddlers when Frank Sinatra gave his last concert, were so interested in his long obituary. All the sponsors at the other tables sounded as if they just wanted to talk about whether it was going to rain, though in the low hum of lunch Jim couldn't really hear any of the words. Maybe when you get to the stage of buying giant-sized ibuprofen and walking briskly around the parking lot, rain becomes more important and obituaries less, so that it doesn't matter if somebody important is alive or not; they just fade away, and the closer it gets to you, the less you can talk about it, until the whole topic reduces itself to a kind of fog that you move through, trying not to call attention to it, a shapeless quality of air like the blended fragrances of the bus.

Jim tried to read the Sinatra story upside down, but it was on the same page as more color pictures of cars on fire. It was impossible not to look at the little riot-stricken vehicles, a kind they don't sell in the States, the faces of the cars more compact, small grille and headlight squeezed together— cute almost, like bumper cars—and everything wrapped in computer-enhanced yellow and orange, so hot that the tires had gone flat.

Maybe it's a fact of life that if you want to find out about Frank Sinatra, you also have to read about young males burning people to death in the street. Jim realized immediately that this was the kind of racist thought that a music department chair, even in a third-tier performance education program that nobody outside Kansas had ever heard of, could put himself at risk for thinking—especially since it disregards all the great composers that non-Western cultures have given to the world.

Another good sign—like real musicians they only talked about their instruments, about which of them had a Peter Eaton, and who had to settle for a Morioka, with its famously smooth key action and its equally famous record-length hold times in the customer service department.

"I had to wait one time for an *hour*," a tired-looking longhaired kid with a soft southern accent said. "And no 800 number either.

Finally this girl picks up: 'Sorry, you have the wrong department.' *Click!*"

"Just like Microsoft," Jim said, tasting the 1890 soup, thick and brown as porridge and so salty he hoped the old people weren't eating too much of it—but then of course he wasn't supposed to have it either.

"But you have to admit one thing," Jim said, scanning from face to face and waxing serious among the lunch sounds. "With all the troubles in the world, you have to admit that the music most companies play when you're on hold is getting better and better."

He got a good laugh out of that one, and he didn't have to confess to these kids that he'd been telling that joke to classes for two years.

"So where are you from?" Jim asked a flannel-shirted boy at the other side of the table.

"Oh, I'm not in the competition," he said and leaned toward the shorthaired girl to his right. "I'm with Lisa. We drove up from Cleveland."

"Don't touch them or you'll get a shock," the southern boy said. "They live in an iron house."

"Not iron," the young woman said, her face brightening as if it were her favorite topic. "It's a *steel* house."

"Like a trailer?"

"No, steel framed," she said. "A real house. Steel joists, steel wall verticals. Even steel webbing to hold the plaster."

Her flannel-shirted boyfriend stared down into his thick soup. "One company put up a bunch of them in Ohio in the forties. Didn't quite catch on, but it's all right."

"How is it to heat?" Jim said and immediately realized that it was an older person kind of question. They both made a sort of mechanical pained laugh.

"We don't *talk* about that," Lisa said. She had a way of finishing a phrase, slamming down hard at the end of it, and then her black eyes would fix on whomever she was talking to.

When the mutton-and-giblet pie came, they had to put away the pictures of cars on fire, and the background hum of voices lowered.

"But no mice!" she said. "We figured out that they can feel something in the *magnetism*!"

When you have listened for years to intermediate and advanced woodwind students—their attack on a note, their decay at the end of a phrase—you begin to understand that there are as many different clarinet voices as there are speaking voices. And there she was, Number 17, couldn't be anyone else, with the Scriabin and the slammed down keys, which he ended up not taking any points off for. In about six hours he was going to stand up there and give her twenty-five thousand dollars, a happy secret to carry through lunch—unless he was wrong, and if he was wrong, it would mean that he should get a job as a cab driver because everything he knew about music was wrong.

She wasn't all that pretty, but somehow everything about her fit together like the instruments in a woodwind quartet—her short hair falling at a diagonal across one side of her face, a way of focusing her dark eyes hard on whomever she was speaking to, and a voice that slammed down at the end of a sentence just the way she slammed down at the end of a musical phrase. Jim tried to imagine what her face would look like at the banquet tonight when he opened the final envelope.

* * *

As people wandered into the expanded ballroom, Jim saw Gwen Stockland and some of the sustaining members standing near the head banquet table close to an older woman who talked to them in a low voice.

She was about seventy, but she had her white hair in braids coiled around on the top of her head, like what you see on girls working in a health food store.

"She's a friend of Kurt VanSickle," Gwen said, taking Jim's arm as she led him around the side of the head table. "He woke up from a nap this afternoon, and he'd suddenly lost the ability to swallow."

"My God," Jim said. "Do they know what's wrong?"

"No. All she said was that they're feeding him with a tube and that he's in no immediate danger."

Jim sat down at his place next to Gwen while the student waitresses poured ice water and brought around the usual little wet salads on flat glass plates. When you think about swallowing and when you realize how that process involves every muscle in the whole throat, you can imagine how somebody could one day just forget how to do it. Jim sat there, thinking about it every time he took a mouthful, moving his head so that he could make the muscles push in the right place easily without having the cartilage of his throat buckle against itself. It's not that hard to do when there's food in your mouth, but to swallow when your mouth is empty, especially when you're thinking about it, becomes almost a trick.

No announcement was made about Kurt VanSickle, but Jim could feel the news of it go around from table to table, a different note in the crowd talk, as if the ceiling had been lowered. At their two tables the contestants sat almost motionless, with a low hum of their own. Gwen and Jim had gone over the winners, and he was right about Lisa being Number 17.

Over the main course choices of raspberry pork loin or vegetarian soufflé, they had entertainment by the University Bassoon Quartet. They were very good, but something about the level of midrange noise in the background made their carefully arranged four-part intervals come out a little cross-modulated, with the slight growl of a wolf tone audible whenever the ensemble re-turned to the tonic G-flat chord.

As in most contests he'd been to, judging was done Miss America style, with Jim as Bert Parks and the ones who didn't win anything getting a big round of applause first, leaving the five finalists standing up in their places around the two tables, almost visibly trembling.

It was strange to stand up there with the envelopes and have nothing be a surprise. He read the names and handed the envelopes out, swallowing once or twice after each one, as if to test out his reflexes, which he knew was just a way to make himself nervous. You don't need to test yourself. When the time comes when you can't swallow anymore, you'll know it.

He announced number five, then four, and three. When he called out the name of the first runner-up, Lisa was left standing there as grand prize winner, and he could see it come over her face as she realized; her mouth fell open and her dark eyes lit up. As she walked up to the podium, almost unsteadily in her heavy raised shoes, Jim could see that, just like Miss America, she was even beginning to cry.

After the winners and the rest of the contestants had milled around hugging each other, everybody sat back down for dessert, which was accompanied by a poetry presentation from the editor of the *Central Michigan Arts Review*, one of the sponsors of this competition. He was a smallish guy about Jim's age, with a beard so bushy that there didn't seem to be an opening anywhere for food.

He read a number of poems from his newest book, *Triangulating the Rain-Scats*, all about growing up in British Columbia. He read them with much lyricism over the soft clinking of good hotel dishware, his voice strong and even and obviously influenced by having been to many poetry readings, because he had picked up the technique of breaking the lines off and leaving them hanging, with a lilting caesura, in the middle of a phrase:

> dawnshine wet on the backs of banana-
> slugs ...

What seemed strange to Jim, sitting two places to the left of the podium, where the reader had placed a pile of the thin pa-perbacks he was going to be selling and signing, was that every one of this guy's poems ended up with people being attacked by bears. Kids were still getting up to hug Lisa, and she sat there glowing, galvanized, as if picking up static electricity from her steel house. A boy is picking blueberries, and a grizzly bear comes loping down the hill toward him. A bear discovers some people's tent in the middle of the night and

> sweeps it free of the land with one
> wipe of its massive paw.

then drags it, with the honeymoon couple still inside, into a tributary of the Fraser River. A bear caught an art student from the University of Toronto and held her down on the ground under him for four hours, and now everything she paints has two big eyes staring out of the canvas.

Flying out to banquets like these was always a luxury to Jim, because once you've done what you're there for and handed out twenty-five thousand dollars to a beautiful girl who lives in a steel house, you can just sit back and listen to poems about people getting killed by bears and watch the kids who didn't win anything hugging the ones who did. And they meant it too, you could see—these good-hearted clarinet players, the salt of the musical earth, not like those prickly, high-maintenance violin geniuses he had to work with sometimes when one of the string competitions wanted a co-judge from a different instrumental group. You can sit there and pick at your dessert and think about the girl who won, her life with her boyfriend, her clarinet arpeggios ringing through the steel house. And although she was not quite beautiful, it was hard not to think about what would happen tonight, when they got home to those joists and I beams.

Bear trouble just leads to more bear trouble: that's a poetic truism. Jim was no literary critic, but he knew enough to know that he wasn't going to buy this guy's book. Although it's not quite appropriate to be sitting there at the dais having mildly erotic fantasies about a student you've barely met, it's better than having to think too closely about getting your legs bitten off. Human nature dictates that when a young woman gets home from winning a clarinet contest, even if it's the middle of the night, she will want to celebrate, meaning that, to put it privately, in the context of a vocabulary Jim was not in the habit of allowing himself to use, she is going to get fucked. It even sounded a little strange when he silently thought the word, because he never used it in public and hardly ever in private, not even when he fluffed a note practicing.

All this time, as they were finishing dessert, the man's voice went on, clear and even, from under the duck blind of beard this time about a tourist family who had watched too many Yogi Bear cartoons:

> still light enough for
> pictures, the bear at the picnic
> table, tame as a dog, he tongued
> marshmallows from their
> fingers, one last snapshot, timed
> perfectly, to catch one
> moment, of a bear eating
> their daughter's hands.

This was as good a time as any to push away the coffee-flavored cheesecake he didn't like much anyway and let his eyes blur over in the direction of the clarinet kids, with Lisa still in the middle, glowing and hugging. If you don't want to listen to somebody's bear attack poems you have to think about something. It's a bad habit to use vulgar language, even in your own mind, when you are thinking about somebody who is that good a clarinet player, but he couldn't stop.

At least it kept him from testing whether he could still swallow. He imagined the girders of that house in the middle of the night, maybe a thunderstorm, and they get home, probably in a crummy old student car. You have to admit that it's relatively harmless to think about the fact that even if she is tired, she will be doing that thing that's best described, when no one is listening, as getting fucked, which a friend of Jim's in the English department once pointed out was the only verb that sounds better in the passive voice, whoever it was that actually got to do it, even if that boyfriend of hers in the flannel shirt didn't seem all that articulate.

If you think hard enough, you can block everything out. Bears may come and bears may go. Jim once read something by a psychiatrist named Viktor Frankl, who said something to the effect that people need to become more aware of the range of choices they have about how they will feel about whatever happens to them and to their friends and families, even when they are being killed by a bear. Jim knew that if he could be in control of that choice, he would look like a god up at the head table, eyes half closed with the imagery, waxing eloquent to himself, about such things as the fact that in some still-memorable respects, the world is a beautiful place, especially when girls are getting ready to go home and have sex during a thunderstorm, which you have to say will help her get primed for her upcoming audition with the Grand Rapids Chamber Orchestra, which is included with first prize. Maybe they will do it three times, which would also be a good thing, if they can manage it, even if her boyfriend is not very articulate, and when you think about what you hope they are going to do at least three times, you realize that the passive voice really does make it more beautiful, when you say it to yourself and never to anybody else, with the right emphasis: that she is getting fucked, fucked, fucked.

Jim always liked the way the person at the podium at the end of a reading takes a last pause and then says "thank you." He clapped hard for the guy with hands trained from going to so many great concerts, making a loud pop, maybe louder than usual because it was a way of thanking him for being finished.

Soon everybody was standing up. Waitresses were busing plates and silverware into tubs on rolling frames. Gwen Stockland was talking to Kurt VanSickle's friend, holding both of the older woman's hands in hers.

Within a few minutes, some of the sustaining members were already beginning to gather around the elevators, going upstairs to bed. With his early flight tomorrow, Jim would have to do the same thing, as soon as he had thanked Gwen and had her give his best wishes to Kurt and then spoken at least briefly to the poet and congratulated all the contestants and double-checked the time with the young woman graduate student who would be driving him to the airport.

As he wandered around the ballroom looking for the graduate student, whose face he could only slightly remember, he thought about some of the man's bear imagery, which seemed to linger in the air of the ballroom, a sour note maybe for the program planners to have ended on, hanging over the little groups of people talking in low voices, a chilly, enduring odor among all the other gathered fragrances.

Or maybe he wasn't entitled to have negative thoughts about an art form that wasn't his. When images stick in your mind like that, it's supposed to indicate that they are well written. Maybe the real story about these poems was similar to what Mark Twain said about Wagner's music: that it's better than it sounds. He was glad at least that they had all been written in free verse, which meant that he didn't have to worry about any of the individual lines or stanzas getting lodged in his memory and playing over and over in his mind tomorrow during the two short flights home.

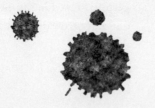

a lover's
guide to hospitals

In my oldest fantasy, everything is perfect after the giant bicycle accident. My friends and I clench our teeth as if imitating sharks, all our appendixes ruptured, such a crowd of us that they have had to call a second ambulance. The pain weighs us down on our stretchers as cleanly as a bag of sand. We are all *injured*, a good strong word from *The Adventures of Rin Tin Tin*, as we drift in white vehicles toward the great white floodlit face of the hospital.

I suppose that now, supported by my barely sufficient graduate student insurance, I'm the closest I'll ever come to that fantasy. But unlike the structures I used to dream about, grand hospitals with their square and dignified faces looking out over districts of residential greenery, this is just a community hospital, set like a pumping station against the riverbank, windows sealed against this valley's moist heat. The pain I feel is something awkward, off balance, tilting toward nausea, something I can't quite get the rest of my body around. Its drug-dulled, destabilized ache is almost lost beneath the continuing swoon of relief that came with what I was told this afternoon—that I still have two testicles and have been delivered of merely a benign cyst.

In the old dream that I loved so much, we waved back and forth between ambulances. I would like to do something like that now, but there's nobody to wave to, and I don't feel well enough. When you love hospitals as much as I do, it's easy to forget that the reason we go into them usually spoils the luxurious emptiness of the time we spend there. Even the shapes of the nurses seem harsh in their bleached white. It has been said that youth is wasted on the young; I guess you could say hospitals are wasted on the sick.

But I have had a second piece of good news: I actually know one of the nurses here. We worked together in the Buckeye Lounge when she was still a medical student. *Still*—that's the important word, for in a town like ours, the law requires that even a strongly ambitious woman dramatically lower her career goals, so as to keep them more in line with those of whatever local carpenter or tinsmith such a woman invariably marries. I like to put things in terms of laws and theories, because in a valley full of those people whose cars and trucks surround this sealed capsule of a hospital, I can talk to myself knowing that if they heard me they would never understand a word.

So Leslie dropped out of medical school (you could say it "came to pass") because she was in love with a gentle, generic, cigarette-smoking fashioner of gentle porcelain objects and so became a nurse instead, for which I have no right to criticize her, which brought her here, to the only hospital in town.

* * *

And as long as I have all this time to fantasize, I might as well think about my other favorite fantasy nurse—Nurse Danko of *The Rookies,* Kate Jackson's first prime-time role. Nurse Danko was that Platonic nurse construct of which real nurses are but shadows on a cave wall. Every time someone got injured (and many were injured but few killed in those kind and violent seventies), he always ended up in Nurse Danko's hospital, and Nurse Danko was always on duty and was always his nurse.

It is significant to me that Leslie looks more than a little like Nurse Danko—the same dark hair, the same keen face, precise without being prim, soft without being sentimental. Lacking Kate Jackson's on-set stylist to comb her out between takes, Leslie had to opt, in the Buckeye Lounge at least, for a single short pigtail.

* * *

What I love about the hospital is that except for during visiting hours, it's an area free of people in pickup trucks. Even the janitors don't have them. I can't think of another place to better shut yourself away from such people—though I know I'm not being fair—from their mindless good luck, away from that sensibility that understands nothing but has a bumper sticker for everything. I love that the windows don't open, that a truck with a bad exhaust system can climb the hill on the other side of Silver Creek, and I won't hear anything but the long afternoon hush of a hospital, a calm yet agitated equilibrium, that gentle bounciness of background nonmusic for which years of soap opera have secretly prepared us.

The night is even better. From my window last night, still at risk, still under the hazard of . . . orchiectomy (a word I had never heard before but knew enough Greek vocabulary to know immediately what it meant and that it was already a word I did not like), I could see what must be a storage room in another wing of the hospital, a chamber full of such a deep, late-night blue light that I didn't know it was possible for anybody on so much medication to wake up at such an hour. No metaphor; that was it: the middle of the night. If you wake up in a hospital, it is wonderful to know that things go on all night, that the republic endures out in its dark fields (whoever it was that said that) and that somewhere a nurse is counting tablets onto a plastic tray.

Even the nonprofessional staff members of this hospital have a kind of delicate unsqueamishness that could never squeeze itself into a one-size-fits-all cap. The faces of the orderlies are calm, even living as they do with the chance that somebody they are talking to will die under the knife, as happens sometimes, in rooms full of delicate electronic objects.

How strange, on a warm afternoon, to think of the two populations of our moist valley separated by the crosshatched glass of the emergency room. On the business side of the partition, the young girls have become so good at filling in the emergency admission forms that the wheezing speed of everything around them hums down a notch.

On the other side of the glass, the patients and their families wait with hurt knees, bleeding hands, reactions to bee stings. It is summer and they are angry. It's too crowded. Something is wrong with the weather. They have been shouting from car to car in the Wal-Mart parking lot about how the only thing the government wants to do these days is take money out of your pockets. Whatever it is they believe is going on with those people in Washington, they know it with such certainty that maybe it *has* to be true. The gathered thought of all of it pushes in the same direction, filled with the same sureness as the man from the Taxpayers Coalition for Congressional Term Limits, who every Saturday sets up a petition table in the store's entranceway on the other side of the automatic doors from the old retired guy whose job it is to smile at everybody and say "Thanks for coming to Wal-Mart."

I have been doomed from the start to have trouble with people in vehicles with engines powerful enough to screech their rear wheels when the light changes. It is the way of the world that in the critical days before some graduate student like me, working in a cocktail lounge, gets up the nerve to ask a waitress like Leslie out—that some local artist-cum-masonry contractor (or maybe a drug dealer using the craft as a cover) is going to walk into the bar, in the process of wandering from restaurant to restaurant, looking for waitresses.

The guy was *focused,* tiny eyes fixed on her, his cigarette dim in the bar light. What can I say but that she married him, a maker of gentle porcelain bric-a-brac? What could I do but wish them well? I looked through their registry at JCPenney and I'm sure they liked what I picked out. At those incense-flavored arts and crafts shows, in a booth next to the mountain dulcimer merchants, he makes (or launders) a lot of money. He gives her gentle porcelain jewelry. The only thing he has ever had the energy to tell me in the bar is that business is going great—of course, as are most marginal businesses not related to the actual economy.

We had that conversation back when she was still majoring in neurophysiology. I went to the Little Professor Book Center and ordered something called the *Human Brain Coloring Book* and colored in a few of the early plates, that we might have something to talk about as we restocked the bar glasses. Plate 1-1: Introduction to the Human Brain. *Because I Love Leslie,* I had penciled across the top in several colors. Plate 1-2: Introduction to Brain Structure. *Because I Love Leslie.* Plate 1-4: Organization of the Nervous System. Same reason, improved calligraphy—but we never did end up talking about brain physiology, so I stopped coloring in the plates.

I remember a night when it was already too late. I drove out to see her in Cincinnati, where she lived on the hill of hospitals. We went out to dinner in my rented car; I couldn't let her see my graduate student Honda Civic. The nicest thing she ever did was trust me (a gentleman, with almost all my coursework done) enough to let me sleep on her living-room floor. I didn't know it at the time, but she already knew she was leaving med school to be back in the same town with her fiancé, had already been accepted into the nursing program at Lawrence County Community College.

Never has the world of hospitals been so beautiful, there in the middle of them, in a little garden-apartment building curled up around itself like a fortress in the dangerous part of town. Those hospitals, alive, hummed in their white light: Baptist Memorial, Shriners' Hospital, Beth Israel, their own little country, their own calendar of all-night hospital life. And never has the night run so deep, all night, when I couldn't sleep from all the real coffee we had with dinner.

Once, on top of Baptist Memorial, the helicopter started up, a horrific crescendo for all those radiology residents catching up on sleep. It roared off, and half an hour later it came back, important beyond all sleep. I was happy to be there or anywhere else where I didn't need to pretend I had a prayer of anything working out.

What a pleasure it was, without sleep the next morning, to kiss her good-bye and tell her I loved her and drive home actually crying from time to time behind sunglasses in a rental car that at least I was not embarrassed by. What a pleasure it was, tired, in my best herringbone sport coat, to stop at the truck stop halfway between our two mutually invisible cities in August, to sulk silent and well dressed in the air-conditioning over my fish sandwich, not knowing if the waitress saw me.

* * *

It was only a few weeks later that I ran into her in MacGoogle-burger's. She was dancing to an anti-Semitic New Age band that neither of us liked much. She was already married by then. I took her hand as I talked to her, gently, unlike the drunks we both knew so well, who grab you by the arms and exhale in your face.

"Leslie, I have something to ask you," I said, and she looked me in the eyes and listened because she already knew I was a gentleman, drunk or sober.

"When you've decided on your nursing specialty"—this shouted close to her hair over a pseudo–Jackson Browne refrain about homeless Palestinians—"please tell me what it is, because whatever your specialty is, I'll be willing to get that disease on the condition that you'll be my nurse."

"Oh, Carl, that's sweet."

"I mean it," I said, twice, and I think she heard me.

"That's really sweet."

"My only request," I said to her, "is that you won't go into oncology." That continues to be my all-time favorite moment between us, because it is the kind of joke that only a man who knows what the word "oncology" means can tell to a woman who knows what the word "oncology" means and whose husband without question does not know what the word "oncology" means. And though he sprawls upon her body nine times a week, with his mustache particulates pungent as an ashtray—and I might as well bring it out into the open that he almost certainly is making her gasp with his tireless, doggish, no doubt uncir-cumcised, thrusts—still, the two of them belong to two different nations: the people who look up words in the dictionary and the people who don't. I'm not afraid to admit that I belong to that population unable to dwindle themselves down far enough to believe in the same God who protects all those filter-tip folk who go through life blessed against cancer, their cigarette smoke drifting over to the no-smoking tables. Two nations. What Leslie and I, and no one else, have had between us amounts to nothing less than a unit of human knowledge. Her husband must bend forward with his cigarette to follow along with infomercials for political third parties, as they grow old together.

* * *

I lay on a tall bed beside a window in a little room on the first floor of the hospital. The anesthesiologist was joking around about something. Rock and roll was playing over the radio, which seemed so strange in a hospital that I thought it meant I was going to die. How right to be swept up in that music when you have something to be afraid of, electric like metal under the tongue, a song with fear in the notes themselves; how beautiful to be swallowed up in this, in the middle of the summer, behind sealed windows with black gaskets around the edges, looking out from the surgery and radiology level into a thicket of green weeds as you plunge asleep.

* * *

For a long time after I woke up, my doctor didn't come around, and I didn't know how many balls I had. It's not the kind of thing I wanted to ask a nurse, even though one of them kept coming in and pulling my covers up.

Now, every half hour, it's a different nurse looking under the covers. Now that I know I'm all right, it makes me proud for some reason to be examined this way. It is the luxury of pain, I suppose, if that still means anything with the drugs we have access to. The old dignity of a wounded bicyclist. The weirdness of that inch of glass, as if in a submarine, between our world inside and the land of bad mufflers outside. There seems to be no connection between us and the scene out there: the bridge over the little river, nothing but cars all day, not a walking figure since I checked myself in.

I have almost given up on Leslie ever coming around when suddenly she walks into the room and stands there for a moment with her face in that tight smile I remember so well from the time I told her I would be willing to get sick.

It is the first time I have seen her in uniform. I used to think that black was the most beautiful color on a woman, but now I know, at once and forever and beyond question, that it's white. The shadow of it clarifies the gradations of her skin color and funnels my attention up to the hard blue of her eyes. My attention is drawn there so quickly that at first I don't notice that she has her hair pinned back—a bit severely, it seems to me—under her white cap.

"Well hi, Carl," she says, and immediately I remember how strong my painkillers are, like jellyfish over my face as I try to talk. I don't know if this is just a social visit or if I'm on her watch.

"Hello Leslie, it's ... really good to see you." What a privilege to be allowed to talk slowly and to know that she'll still be listening at the end of the sentence, such as it is.

I don't know what I expected with the hair. Nurses always have their hair pinned. The only place you see nurses wearing their hair loose is in a porno movie. She must be on an official visit, because she does what all the other nurses have done. She pulls away the sheets, lifts my gown, and stares mildly at the wounds I haven't seen yet. I lie there in the mild white of this room, my dark bruises bathed in the reflection of her uniform, which throws white light off of itself as if we are in a commercial for Clorox 2, its brightness overpowering the greenish cloud shadows outside.

And there she is above me, locked away forever in her gentle porcelain marriage, her clear features uncomplicated by anything but the fact of how beautiful she will remain for the next few years, until she gets hard and fat and has to quit her job for babies. For now, at least, I am sick and she is my nurse. I am more than sick; I am *injured.* And somehow, as if I am again nine years old and imagining myself groaning bravely in the ambulance, somehow the condition of being injured brings me close to being as perfect in my fashion as she is in hers, leaving me half exposed on the bed in front of her, with a plastic thunder mug hooked over the bar at the side of the bed, yet more of a man, I would like to think, than her eternal, unblemished, nicotine, coitus partner.

If this were an episode of *The Rookies,* this would be the moment they freeze the frame and roll credits. She helps me sit up and lets me see for the first time the dark bruise of my numbed intactness, and I feel a kind of triumph fill the little room—which I still have to pay twenty percent of—but then with this much Percodan, everything feels like triumph. The sun comes out, far away outside the glass, around it a polarized rainbow.

Even her teeth are perfect as victory radiates out into the un-air-conditioned world. I can imagine that everybody who has ever taken anything I loved away from me is trapped out there in the open and can't get into the shade, their moles and freckles mutating in the sun. One by one, the third-party rallies disperse, still angry but not sure what about; credit cards come up declined at gas pumps; and all over America the bumper stickers, even those put on just last week, have begun peeling away like old Band-Aids when there is no cut underneath.

in a city with dogs

Other than a man I used to know from school who was collecting signatures on a petition to abolish the international police force, and the kid in Central Park who tried to rob me by saying he had a gun built into the shoe of his artificial leg, my memories of the months I lived in New York are more or less unpopulated. I know that I remember the dogs better than I remember the people—how the long patient faces of dogs being walked across the honeycomb pattern of hexagons in the pavement around the Museum of Natural History seemed every day to grow calmer, more detailed, more tolerant of their masters' overloaded schedules.

Perhaps I could say it was the worst time of my life—all those sleepless hours in bed with no air conditioner, while boom boxes playing disco music moved slowly past the open window of my ground floor apartment, and those walks along Broadway through the airborne scraps of trash, as I composed over and over the letter I would write to the *Times* in response to someone else's letter.

But now, when I remember those days in my apartment with the curtains pulled, I feel the same warmth that I feel when I think about the time a few years later when my insurance company allowed me to spend two nights in the hospital for what ordinarily would have been ambulatory surgery, because I had made the excuse that I had nobody to take care of me. I lay awake watching the steady, all-night quality of light in the hall, through which the shadows of nurses, silent on their white cork shoes, passed from time to time, in secret, the way the tires of taxis used to pass outside my apartment window when I was not quite asleep. Never has a city so opened itself to me, taking me in and giving me a place to walk around and around in the middle of the day, and never have I so opened myself to a city, let it take hold of me and shake me upside down, although we had nothing to offer each other beyond the fact of being relentlessly, in the expression that was gaining currency at the time, in each other's faces.

But faces are what I remember least. I have no idea what my sister's friends looked like, although I had dinner with them twice and once walked in circles with them beneath the tall pines in Pelham Bay Park, our heads tilted back on our shoulders, looking for owls.

I do remember the flag on their wall, from what country I did not ask: horizontal bars running above and below a central figure that looked like the transverse of a dime, everything in the same shades of yellow and brown and orange that I would see a few years later in the bumper stickers of parked cars when I drove past the local community college.

I remember summer better than I remember winter, day better than night, and the white litter of Broadway flying waist high when the wind picked up. The strange thing about being in New York is that even when you take time away from it, for a day or a weekend, you're still there. You can walk down a neighborhood street in New Jersey, with kids playing in every other yard and the horizon low to the ground in all directions, or you can watch the dining-room window darken from a Thanksgiving table in Connecticut, and you're still stuck in New York. Never has a city so taken me in, so swallowed me up whenever I came back to it, the outline of the midtown buildings growing taller in the blue haze as we approached them diagonally on the Carey Airport Express bus.

* * *

With nothing to put into it, time loses all shape, so that whatever I did over those long days I seemed scarcely able to fit into the hours available. Once I made a series of expensive daytime phone calls to Merv Griffin Productions to register my disagreement with the way *Timbuktu* had been spelled on *Wheel of Fortune*. I thumbed through the Manhattan Yellow Pages, and wherever an ad included a picture of the New York skyline, I drew a little cartoon H-bomb streaking down onto it. I walked and walked, never very far from my own neighborhood, watching how gently the sun fell on all the other people who were not working, watching how it glanced off the window of the Holistic Pet Care Center, where cats sprawled asleep among the carpeted plywood shapes of scratching posts and nesting boxes.

At the International Auto Show, I walked for hours among the displays, up and down the Coliseum's long ramp, wondering if I was the only city person there among the tailored jeans and suede jackets of those who could think seriously about owning such vehicles—people who lived someplace where you could look straight ahead or right or left and there would be lawns and trees and places to park. I watched as the automobiles turned slowly on felt-covered turntables, each exhibit attended by a young woman with her face contoured by carefully applied makeup. The smiles of the models were mirrored in the hard wax of the cars, their lip gloss reflecting the same fluctuating lights that danced on the cars' dark quarter panels. All that day I longed for the suburbs—their open-skied subdivisions, their sprawling, pasted-together high schools, built one wing at a time over twenty years, with empty football bleachers visible from the New Jersey Turnpike on the kind of Sunday through which you can drive for hours without ever seeing a person on foot.

* * *

From my bedroom on the ground floor I could see, thrown onto a small area of the ceiling, the vague shapes of people and objects moving outside. Like the pinhole viewers that schoolchildren build to safely watch an eclipse, the gap at the top of my window where the curtains did not quite come together would throw onto my ceiling a blurred picture of people and vehicles passing outside: the yellow sweep of a taxi making a half-circle across the small projection area near the pinhole; the tiny figure of someone in a red shirt scissoring across the ceiling in the direction opposite from the way the person was actually walking. I would think of all the dogs being walked in the sunlight—how beautiful they were with their calm, tolerant faces and the white parts of their fur somehow whiter than anything else in the city—and sometimes I would go outside just to see them.

Coming home, I would usually stop at a small grocery store on Columbus Avenue. What a vacancy it was to walk, without a job and without anybody telling me to start looking for a job, into the shadowy cramped spaces of that store, into its stale banana smells and cheese smells and the smell of the powdery duff of sawdust and dried onion skins and miscellaneous half-dehydrated vegetable residue that collected, out of reach of the push broom, in the cracks between the floorboards.

Everything was close together—the round grapefruits gathered in their net bags; crowds of heavy and dim-colored vegetables, whose names and uses I did not know, framed in shallow boxes forming a slanted flat surface; the soda bottles upright in the cooler, jammed together so closely that it was hard to reach in without something falling out. What simplicity to walk home with the groceries, in sunglasses, with oranges and a quart of ginger ale, on the hottest day of the year; what an eventless holiday to come home to a building while everybody else was at work, to loosen with a twist the cubes in a plastic ice tray and pour them into a waxy green Tupperware bowl, perhaps cradling a few cubes in the palm of my hand and cracking them into two or three smaller pieces with the handle of a steak knife, and to sip ginger ale in a room without a fan, where I had never even thought about getting a fan, sitting back in my one comfortable chair with ink-darkened channels worn into its armrests from hours of running a ballpoint pen back and forth along the grain of the wood, sitting still in the almost motionless apartment air, which blended sometimes with a breath of the moist, clean smell of my white tile bathroom. I always got the kind of oranges with the thickest skin, so I could squeeze the skin next to a match flame and watch the volatile oils flare up, again and again, sometimes in a remarkably large burst of fire. Soon the air would be filled with black motes of carbon from the burned oil: wispy, wormy shapes spiraling and drifting in the slight turbulence that the heat from the flare-ups had generated.

What a lazy smell on a summer afternoon—the air sharp with sulfur and burned orange oil, and the metallic ozone refrigerator smell of ice cubes melting in the plastic bowl—while the gesticulating images of people outside crossed my ceiling and the taxis flashed past, throwing a fan of yellow through the pinhole.

* * *

There is no privacy deeper than the privacy of sunglasses. I could walk however many blocks in whatever direction I found myself going, then turn, perhaps, and cross at a light and walk in some other direction. I could watch the beautiful dogs with their adult faces, who seemed to have come to terms with the burden of heat that wrapped itself around their unsheddable coats, watch in the thick sunlight among the brick buildings the slim people who had somehow provided room in their lives for dogs, and think how after dark the dense red bricks would radiate back into the street the heat they had absorbed all day. One corner seemed the same as any other, one hour the same as any hour, among the masonry, among the moving pastels of shorts and tank tops in colors that were so much easier to remember than the faces of the people who wore them. What puzzles me most is how fervently I told myself over and over again that I hated those days. I even had a spiral notebook lined with blank staffs of music in which I wrote little jingles about how terrible everything was: the year, the city, even myself, behind sunglasses, walking slowly along streets full of dogs, with the rest of the day sprawled out in front of me, at once empty and booked solid as a doctor's office, the hours shapeless and swollen beyond all consideration of getting anything done within their sleepy and breezeless schedule.

a bend
among bumblebees

We're sitting there waiting for our fake margaritas when we hear that sneezing noise of a charter bus pumping its air brakes, and in about half a minute *La Sombrero* is wall-to-wall with green warm-up jackets from one of those flag twirling and color guard squads that were competing this weekend at the HeiferDome. This group is called the Bradfield Bumblebees. You should have seen them. Their jackets were such an intense acid green that it reflected off the ceiling.

We're pretty near the door, at the table where we usually sit. Deb and I are already a little punchy, and Katy's catching up. When the three of us were having dinner across the street at Julia's Pantry, we'd been laughing about the same magazine article most of you probably saw. I mean, talk about wide coverage. It's in dentist's offices and everything.

When the three of us were over in Julia's, I'd gotten both of them laughing about some spinach and lamb sausages I was having. This is crude, I admit, but the resemblance to what the magazine was talking about was close enough to notice. I held one out on my fork—balanced, not speared, I promise—and I said, "Would you like a personal attribute?"

This caught Deb with wine in her mouth. She had to catch it with a napkin to keep from dripping on the white table-cloth—not that Julia's is all that stuffy, but Martha Stewart says you shouldn't do a spit-take with Bordeaux.

I'd just gotten back into town, a day late, because I missed my connection on the way back from seeing Geoff in Phoenix. His contracting business is going well enough that he could send me a ticket, which was great, except that when he was bringing me back to the airport, his pickup truck stalled in the passenger drop-off area, and he couldn't get it started. Of course the airport police were all over him. I couldn't do anything; I had to check in for the flight.

Then when I get to Denver, my bag makes the connection, but I don't—that's a reversal—and the airline decides to shuttle us halfway across town and put us up in a Radisson next to the University of Denver, so there I am with no suitcase and nothing but that nasty little toilet kit they give you.

Big holiday. Outside my door a bunch of college kids are thumping up and down the corridor, the guys yelling, "Trick or Treat!" and the girls saying "Shut up!" I could hear that through the door. I was so bored that I spent five minutes looking through the security hole watching them go back and forth.

Funny thing about Halloween in a college; I never thought about it around here until I went away and noticed it somewhere else. Have you ever noticed the girls' costumes, what a production some of them make of it, dressed and made up like hookers, or belly dancers, or Cleopatra, with gold breastplates and tassels and everything?

It's too bad, really. Even the prettiest girls realize that they're obligated to go clumping around campus day after day with the same flannel shirt hanging out from underneath the same old sweater. The good old casual look. The only time they can experiment with looking pretty is that one night a year. Well, I guess I'm worse. I don't even do that much.

So there I was up in my room all night, which is iambic pentameter, and I've got no nightgown, which is fine when Geoff's there, but the rest of the time I'm just not used to it—and I know you're all interested in the details of my private life. Really, it's just these little Reese's Peanut Butter Cups talking. You know how modest I am in real life. If people wouldn't put all their Halloween leftovers out here in the coffee room every year, I'd never get this way.

Anyway, the cheerleaders, flag-flappers, keep milling around in the *Sombrero*. There's not a man in the group. In fact, there's not a male in the whole restaurant, except maybe whoever is in the kitchen, just Deb and Katy and me and the two overworked waitresses scrambling around from table to table and these twenty-five or so girls and two older women chaperones. There was so much green in that room from their jackets that—I don't know what. Somebody else come up with a metaphor. I'm too full of sugar to think straight.

Pretty soon the three of us at our margarita table are back on the personal presidential attribute topic. Great topic, sitting around wondering what something like that looks like. I mean it's somebody in public life. Meaning everything is public, I guess. Out at the curb, the bus keeps trying to do something, to blow the moisture out of its air brakes or something.

For a while the girls around us can't hear anything. But with a subject like that, it's hard for certain words not to get really clear when you hear them a few times. And then something Deb said must have coincided with the quietest part of the Mexican elevator music tape that Gary always plays over and over again on the restaurant sound system, so that she finishes up making a point that ends, not loud, but very emphatically, with a very *clinical* word, I won't say it, and suddenly every conversation stops, and the only sound in the place is *"Guantanamera"* on soft guitars.

The girls are staring, trying to be polite, looking halfway over at us, the way people did with that linguistics experiment they forced me to do in graduate school, where I had to go up to people on the street and see how they reacted when I said, "Colorless green ideas sleep furiously."

Speaking of words that don't go together, I hope you all know that at least somebody in this town tried to get Gary to change *La Sombrero* to *El Sombrero*. You know I went out with Gary for a while, and I sat there with him in his pickup truck many times, *trying* to explain how some languages other than English have grammatical gender. He's not a stupid person, but I guess the only gender he ever understood was the gender of his own—well, I won't say that either. You can tell everybody that Jeannie's on a Reese's Peanut Butter Cup buzz and in five more minutes, if they time it right, she's going to be talking dirty.

I tried to make him understand that, if nothing else, it's going to sound really retarded to Spanish people and even to kids here who take Spanish, but maybe he's right—who cares? Where are those Spanish people? If you put up a sign in the window of your business, it doesn't matter where the apostrophe goes; all that matters is that kids walking by can tell whether or not the place is hiring on the day shift.

So I couldn't get through to him, which means that the only thing I have left to be proud of around here is that we're the only town in the state with a phone book that has more doctors listed than chiropractors.

The Bumblebee girls just sit there, making a point of not looking at us talking about CNN and the President's you-know-what, focusing back on their flautas and enchiladas. Nobody's eaten more than a quarter of what's in front of them. Of her. They stare down at their plates, all their faces looking pretty much the same, most blondes, their hair all in the same careful sweep.

Nice kids really; you can see it just by the way they lift the food to their faces. No matter how nasty a place Bradfield is supposed to be—all that stuff on KARO-Land news about the Satanic babysitter, who turned out to be a girl who left an Ozzy Osbourne CD on the parent's sound system—you can look at those girls and it's weird, because they're just cute, that's all you can say. The place and the face don't go together. They're just nice. I know that's a stupid sounding word and students should never use it in their papers because it's too general, but you can say it over and over again, and it's still true; you look at them, and there's none of that Timothy McVeigh reptile stare that you see in the boys. Their eyes all look as if the same makeup artist has worked on them. The lashes are coated with some kind of opaque gel, and they flare out in all directions, which makes the eyeballs look twice as big.

All this time something must be wrong with the bus. It's not humid enough out there for it to keep having to blow the moisture out of its brake lines, or whatever that noise is. It's loud. Deb jumps every time it goes off. She and I are trying to get each other calmed down, because it isn't fair to these kids to make them listen to this personal attribute stuff. I mean, the question comes up: Is he circumcised? Are we entitled to know that? Maybe this will give them ideas that, if they talk about them back at school, will get them suspended from the flag team.

Deb's trying to get back to a normal topic, about the ridiculous vehicle they gave her for the conference and how she had to stop three times and fill out three separate gas vouchers.

But I guess it's a fact of life that when the attribute topic has raised itself, excuse the metaphor, it's hard not to get laughing again. I don't even know who's buying the margaritas now, but there they are—so-called. Since Gary sold the hard liquor part of his license, he can't use any tequila at all, just a kind of lemony wine punch. We shouldn't even bother with them. I know one person in this department who makes them from scratch, and they're ten times as good.

I should have done something to steer Deb back to the gas voucher topic—that's the right metaphor—but I guess Katy and I were both just egging her on. Or something. Can you steer somebody with eggs?

And it's weird especially, for Deb and me definitely, and Katy at least mostly, to be saying things like that about somebody in public life and to live up here in the middle of nothing and not hate him as much as everybody else does, at least not as much as people with bumper stickers that have the first letter of his name forming a communist sickle.

Deb's trying to keep it down to a whisper, but it's getting to be a loud whisper, and she lets it get louder just at the wrong time, when she's getting into it, some sentence that can only end one way, with one word. What can you call it? The Penis Word.

Dead silence. Even the bus has quit blowing its nose. We try to get ourselves back to whispering, but at this point it's hopeless. Even when the Bumblebee girls are talking to each other, we can see that they're bending their ears in our direction.

It doesn't matter by now. We'll embarrass them, and we'll embarrass ourselves, and everybody will be happy. I didn't want this to happen, but now we're getting into measurements. Fox Network said five inches; Headline News said six. CNN gave him a break at six and a half. I hope he appreciated that. And the circumference of a quarter; all three news organizations agreed on that.

I know I should have stopped them. I was the highest ranking person at the table, but I guess I was a little silly by then, if you can believe I'm capable of that, so I just blurt out that five inches doesn't sound that great to me, which of course at that point I'm not quick enough on the uptake to see that that's what Deb was saying in the first place. I said, "I don't mean to brag about my fiancé, but I've had better than that in the last forty-eight hours."

The poor girls, at least the ones close enough to hear us, must be humiliated by now. They're laughing down into their food and sort of choking at the same time.

Next thing you know, Katy reaches into her pocketbook, rummages around, and pulls out two ten-dollar quarter rolls from the Mesaba Flats Indian Casino that she and her husband have been going to.

"You want to know what it looks like?" Katy says. "Let's find out what it looks like. Number one: this here is the exact circumference of a quarter."

She tears the paper off and balances the stack on the table. She says something like she's enough of a chemist to know how to make a model.

"That's five inches?" I say.

She has a tape measure, of course, and she whips it out. Is that the right expression? Anyway it's nowhere near five inches. So she opens the other roll and starts stacking it on top of the first, four coins at a time, dollar by dollar. The kids are looking over, but I don't know if they know what she's doing.

Five inches is more than you'd think—high enough to be a little precarious on one of Gary's wobbly tables when it hasn't been shimmed level with a wadded up matchbook.

Point of information: it took everything except the last five quarters of the second roll to make five inches, for a total of eighteen dollars and seventy-five cents.

Katy's sitting in front of the money, bent over it, cradling the pile as if she's about to put it in her mouth, and for just a minute I get a flash of an old X-rated movie someone took me to once, or showed me; I know it wasn't Geoff.

It must have been this kind of timid guy I used to go out with before I got married for the first time. This guy, Charles, used to say he believed he was under a curse, and he thought that if he ever told me he loved me that I would end up marrying a man in a pickup truck. So he never told me he loved me, just took me to the same restaurant over and over and then tried to get me to watch porno tapes, but they were the nasty kind. If he'd really paid any attention to me, he would have known that there's a whole subgenre of pornography meant for women that he might have gotten me to watch, all gentle and softly lit, and I guess no come shots; excuse the expression. You didn't hear me say that. This story is almost over. I have a meeting. Maybe I'll tell the same story to the associate dean. So I ended up marrying a man in a pickup truck anyway. And I'm about to do the same thing a second time. Maybe it's the same curse still working, poor bastard. Maybe he still loves me.

The kids must have figured out what the coins were, because they're making these convulsive shaking movements over their plates, not so much laughing as knocking themselves out trying not to laugh.

I said I was the highest ranking person there, so it was my job to change the subject, but what can you change it to? We've heard about Deb's bus, we've heard about my hotel room. I was a little bit crazy anyway, almost like now. Alcohol, sugar, what's the difference? One little hydrogen atom over in the corner. Even our students would understand that, if they were still required to take chemistry.

But we forgot one thing, and it falls to my exalted rank to be the one to blurt it out.

"What about the *bend*?" I say. "CNN says it's supposed to curve to one side." The girls must know more about things than Bradfield's library is allowed to keep on the shelves, because instantly the ones still sitting down are giggling and choking again and trying not to spit Diet Coke out their noses. Their big-armed woman coach is up at the bar counter paying the bill, and some of the other girls are bunched up near the door. I do think it was a classy touch that the coach, and even the chaperones, had been issued adult sizes of the same Bumblebee jacket.

"I can't do a bend," Katy says, in a loud stage whisper. "It'll fall over." The girls are milling around, watching us from the side, lifting their acid-green jackets from the backs of their chairs.

Then this one girl comes up to our table. Same blonde hair as the others, with this sweet little Wonderbread face and her eyelashes waxed outward like the spokes of a wheel, she comes up to me all serious.

"We're sorry we listened in like that," she said, and then she stood there waiting, as if I were going to give her detention.

It was weird. I'm not psychic, or if I am psychic it's only on All Saint's Day. I almost started to cry. I swear I could look at that girl, at that kid's face, and I could read the whole unfolding story of her life in Bradfield like reading a plot summary out of Cliffs Notes. I could look at her and tell, as surely as I know that in three weeks I'm going to marry another carpenter with another pickup truck, that this girl's going to end up married to a violent alcoholic.

Poor kid. You know what her eyes looked like? I'm not just talking about the makeup. I mean the eyeballs. They looked like those eyes you used to see in the old Japanese cartoons—if you've ever watched them—big trembly black shiny things waiting to be slapped. The husband will have bumper stickers lined up all the way across the back of his pickup truck. We won't have the same president by that time, but he'll be mad enough about somebody else that if he pulls up behind you and you have a bumper sticker for the person he hates, you'd better watch out.

If this had been a real Japanese cartoon, I would have been able to see in the corner of each of her eyes a windowpane-shaped reflection of Headline News over at the far end behind the bar.

I guess I was tired from all that laughing, but God it was sad. I got sad all over again about not seeing Gretchen, thinking of her studying away with a pile of international relations textbooks next to her, in one of those dreary places in Warsaw they call "student hotels," where there's not enough light over the desk to see what you're reading.

And then I'm looking at this poor kid, probably never been out of the state, just waiting for me to yell at her, I guess, because she kept standing there.

I wanted to say "*Run!* Get *out* of here! You're in trouble and you don't even know it. I'll drive you somewhere. I'll give you a plane ticket." But of course I just said something to her like it's okay, don't worry about it, then turned back to the table.

Deb and Katy are going nuts again. Katy had the bend figured out. What she did was slip a couple of dimes between the quarters on one side, to make a sort of crook right in the middle of it, and she kept holding on to both ends of the stack.

Just then I see that there's no line at the bathroom, so this has to be the time or else—another one of those details I know you all like to hear about my urinary life.

Anyway, I get up too fast and bump the table, which bumps Katy's elbows, and she loses her balance with the bend. The whole pile crashes down, and I mean crashes, all those quarters, loud as anything on the wood floor, the whole five inches' worth, however much it added up to, eighteen dollars and seventy-five cents, the coins all clattering and rolling, and then it's dead quiet again.

Kids like these have to be just about the most polite people in the world, but I guess you can't blame them for not trying to help us pick any of it up, considering what it was supposed to be, or to have been.

Gary's music tape, which I think is the same one he had back when we were going out, has cycled back twice in the time we've been there, and now, for either the second or third time, it's on "*Celito Lindo.*" "*Ay, yi, yi, yi!*" The girls aren't saying much, just reaching back with both hands to pull their hair out from under their Bumblebee jackets and fan it out in the air before it falls, in a practiced motion they must have taught each other.

As the group starts moving out to the charter bus, they're trying not to be too obvious about looking over in our direction. We can see that they are walking very gently because there's money all over the floor.

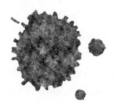

ashes north

Roy's two sons both cried on the phone when Bob finally reached them from the lobby of a pizza restaurant whose main dining area was filled with coin-operated cars and rocket ships. Bob had been calling their house every few hours, not knowing when they would get back from their camping trip.

"So … where is he?" Jim asked, controlling himself, giving the word *he* a kind of humiliated non-emphasis. His usually hale and hearty foghorn of a voice trembled over the phone, as if he was afraid of the answer.

Bob had to tell his nephews that their father was refrigerated and that the funeral home couldn't do anything with the body until they had received written authorization from the next of kin.

Refrigerated must be one of the less comforting funeral home euphemisms—though the people who devised that vocabulary were probably right that to a grieving family the word *frozen* would sound a bit too industrial.

The receiver Bob was talking on had been sprayed with a strawberry-flavored deodorant so strong that he didn't want to put his mouth directly against it, so he had to speak louder than he really wanted to, which made him feel even more conspicuous than usual, in the midst of soft electronic music, wearing the paisley tie and blue cord jacket he still had on from this afternoon's discussion with the lawyers. In summer, around here, anything but shorts would be conspicuous.

The phone stood by itself against the wall of a sort of corral area where parents stood together, and their kids ran around making loops in all directions, some with arms swept back like the wings of a jet. At the place where the corral narrowed to a sort of chute that led to the ordering counter, a tall college boy, with a smile that never changed, marked every hand with an ink stamper, gently lifting even little babies' wrists, as the families were moved through the turnstiles. From there they proceeded toward the kiddie ride area containing dozens of miniature Chitty Chitty Bang Bang cars and Harley-Davidsons, like the stationary rides outside the front door of a supermarket, their headlights gently nodding up and down; or into the room beyond it, full of "Top Gun" and "Terminator" video games and a whole lineup of Skee-Ball setups along one wall; or to the showroom, at the far end of the indoor space, where the human-sized figures of rabbits and chickens, plush as carnival prizes, swiveled back and forth, and a precise electronic chorus of clown voices sang "Happy Birthday" cranked up into a hyperactive 4/4 foxtrot.

The worst thing about making this call was that Bob had to start talking business with these kids, or at least with the older one, right away, while they were still crying. Otherwise he wouldn't be able to leave here, and he'd end up having to drive Roy's Oldsmobile around Fort Pierce for another week, waiting to get the last of his brother's loose ends tied up, having to sleep for another week on the slippery plastic air mattress he'd bought at Kmart after he had Roy's furniture taken away.

Retired people are instinctively supposed to love Florida, but every time Bob got behind the wheel of that loose-springed station wagon, all he could think about was how great he'd feel on the day he got that wallowing boat of a car headed north on I-95. Every time he thought about it, his palms would start to itch on the steering wheel.

Maybe Dorothy had hoped he would love it and would want them to move down. Every time she called him from home, she asked him how the weather was, even though he knew she watched The Weather Channel when he wasn't there.

"Not cold," he would say.

A man who had spent half his life as a salesman should have known better than to die without a will. Bob had tried diplomatically to bring it up with Roy in the hospital one night, during a commercial break.

"Do you have anything specific that you would like me to say to Jim and Rich?" Bob had asked him at one point, but he couldn't even get his brother to turn his face away from the hospital television.

"What, are you trying to get me in the ground already?" he said, and Bob let it drop.

Now he had to pick it up again. The funeral home wouldn't release or cremate the body until the next of kin had sent written authorization, along with a check for storage and cremation costs. As Bob explained this to Jim, he could hear his nephew's voice changing register, very quickly, from tears to anger, the way people have learned to do from watching those afternoon talk shows that were just becoming big in syndication the year Bob retired from the business.

"Let me get this straight," Jim said, and Bob could hear, along with the gathering anger, a family note, a harmonic of the same strong deal closer's voice coming out. Near the phone, somebody's father had just put fifty cents into a game where kids threw beanbags into Bozo the Clown's mouth, and the distant "Happy Birthday" was drowned out by a circus march dizzy with slide trombones. "You say this so-called funeral home won't release the body until we pay them $235?"

"I don't like it either," Bob said. "But without any written instructions, that's how they have to do it." This was as close as Bob wanted to come to getting into a discussion of the word *intestate*.

"So what you're saying is that they're holding my dad's body as a fucking *hostage*?"

With every beanbag throw, no matter how far off it was, the open space of Bozo's mouth boomed positive comments: "That's the spirit, partner!" or "Whoa, Nellie! Good try!"

"Jim, I can't stay down here and fight with these people. If you don't have the money, I'll pay it, but what I do need from you—"

"I'm not paying them, and *you're* not paying them." His voice was rising, a distorted buzz in the earpiece. "Nobody's paying them a goddamn *cent*! Do you fucking *hear me*?"

Bob moved the receiver a few inches from his ear. He could imagine Jim, and his younger brother Rich, on the other end of the line, up there in Pennsylvania, probably in the kitchen of some bungalow with dishes piled in the sink, both of them standing there red-eyed, big, strapping right-wing kids whose father couldn't afford to send them to college and who couldn't get it together to go on their own, any more than they could get it together to hop on a Capitol Air Skybudget flight for the whole three months that they knew their father was down here dying. The last time Bob had seen them, a year ago when he came over to help Roy pack up the station wagon for Florida, the two boys had been working out so much on the Nautilus that they looked as if they were wearing football shoulder pads under their T-shirts.

Jim's voice was out of control now, up to the pitch where people, especially fat people, stand up on camera and point fingers at each other like pistols.

"If those people think they can extort money from me just because I'm too far away to do anything about it, well they can *kiss my motherfucking—*"

Here there was a slam and a crackle over the line, and then the sound clicked through a few switchings of empty channels until it lapsed back into a dial tone, just as Bozo's electronically synthesized drum and trombone music abruptly slammed shut midphrase during "A Hot Time in the Old Town Tonight." "Happy Birthday" had also stopped at the other end of the restaurant, leaving the lobby bathed in a kind of endless chirp in the upper registers, a blend of all the children's voices, not frantic but almost peaceful, like starlings up north when they gather in trees.

His brother had been dead for three days, which was long enough for Bob to start seeing potential jokes popping up in places where they didn't belong. Anybody who has worked in syndicated television or has had anything to do with cartoons knows that what was supposed to happen now was that the phone should ring again immediately, and Bob should pick it up, and he should hear the one word—"*ass!*"—before the phone was slammed down again.

But of course Jim and Rich didn't have the number. Bob accessed MCI again, called, and got a busy signal. It was still busy when he called again two minutes later, and by this time he figured that Jim must have broken the phone.

* * *

Bob was hungry, and the pizza smelled better and better the farther he got from the strawberry fragrance of the phone receiver, but this wasn't the kind of place you'd want to eat. If you sat at a table here without any kids, they'd think you were some kind of weirdo, and they'd be right. You'd have to put some kiddie-sized plates across from you, maybe with half-chewed pizza slices on them, and then people would think you were here with your children (or grandchildren, more likely; most of the parents here, chunky and smooth in pleated shorts and bright collarless T-shirts, looked younger than Bob's own daughters).

People would look at the uneaten slices across from you, and they would think your kids were away from the table rolling Skee-Balls or hunched at the controls of the "Desert Storm" tank simulator—like in the old *Bob Newhart Show* episode where Elliot Carlin had no date for a banquet and draped a woman's sweater over the chair next to him, telling everybody the whole night that she was in the bathroom. Strange how references from the shows he'd been selling all these years to local television stations kept coming into play in the real things he was thinking about. Another sign that he had retired too early.

The people who would have liked this restaurant would have been Roy's family, if such places had existed in the years when he still had a house and a wife and was making enough money to have a little fun with. Jimmie and Richie would have raced around from pachinko to helicopter to the interactive video Kawasaki that actually leaned into the curves, and Roy's big laugh would boom out through the game room, strong as Bozo's.

What a family. When they came to visit at Bob's house, Bob's daughters would hide their better toys from "the Destroyers." Roy loved anything that resembled a party. He was fascinated by comedy record albums, always bringing one or two new ones that he played on Bob's hi-fi, until it was so late at night that Roy was the only one laughing. Then Roy and Maude and the kids would all sleep late into the morning, as Bob's family tiptoed through breakfast.

* * *

Jim called the apartment that night. With all the furniture gone, the sound of the telephone resonated off the Sheetrock walls.

"I'm sorry I lost it like that, Uncle Bob," he said, so softly that Bob had to press the receiver against his ear. "The whole phone was just trashed. I'm sorry it took so long to get back to you."

Roy's little one-bedroom efficiency apartment was bare, the cupboards sponged off, the carpets steam cleaned by a company whose advertising card had come to Roy's mailbox the day he died. Bob had sold back the furniture, the lamps, and even the big splashy oil paintings of city skylines and yacht marinas to the same dealer Roy had bought them from. Bob sat on a metal folding chair under the fluorescent fixture of the kitchen nook, the only place with enough light now to read the paper.

They agreed on a tentative date for a memorial service up north, then moved on to settling the few details that Jim needed to take care of himself. He hardly sounded like the same person who had been shouting so loud on the phone a few hours ago.

Whenever Bob thought about his nephew, he imagined the kid still twelve years old, he and Richie dashing across the garden Bob had just planted. He remembered one time in particular, when the grown-ups were on the porch having drinks, and Jim's voice came bellowing out from the backyard through a megaphone made from rolled poster paper, so loud that the whole neighborhood could hear, "Now hear this! Now hear this! Uncle Bob's scarecrow is on fire!"

* * *

What does a man know about his brother? A big voice, a big handshake, bad luck. When the scrambling to get furniture trucked away slowed down, Bob had ended up with a carload of things he knew nobody wanted, but he didn't dare take responsibility for throwing them out. Whole boxes of monaural comedy albums going back to Shelley Berman. Pay stubs, Social Security statements, handwritten envelopes rubber-banded together, big, glossy folders from something called the Family Bargain Network, describing "Ten Building Blocks on the Horizon of Telemarketing Prosperity." Is building blocks on the horizon a mixed metaphor? Before Roy got sick he'd had a part-time job, working out of the apartment, selling magazine subscriptions by phone. The entire sales pitch was printed out on three glossy pages: "Hi there! Could I speak to the lady of the house, please?"

For the whole year he lived in Florida, even including the three months when he already knew he had cancer, Roy had also been answering personal ads from the back pages of supermarket tabloids. He put a classified advertisement of his own in the same newspaper that said Satan's face had appeared above the White House.

The letters that had come in, always in fountain pen, in careful, grammar school cursive, said things like "Hello, lonely stranger" and "Are you the person I'm looking for?"

The only letter different from the rest was from a young blonde girl who had sent a nude Polaroid, her eyes red from the flash. Bob read a few sentences of her letter, until he came to the code word *generous*.

One of the last things Bob had to do—after he had made sure that Jim was proceeding to ask around and find out where there was a fax machine on which he could send word to the funeral home—was to send some kind of acknowledgment back to all the people who had written to Roy.

It made Bob feel like a bastard, but there were so many people to write to that he had no choice but to answer them with a form letter:

Dear Friend:

I'm sorry to report to you that my brother, Roy Pollard, passed away in Fort Pierce, Florida, on June 28 after a brief illness.

He mentioned several times before he died how much he had been cheered by the kind and friendly mail he had received. Thank you for helping to brighten the last months of his life. In lieu of flowers or condolences, I know that my brother would appreciate contributions made in his name to the American Cancer Society.

Sincerely, Robert R. Pollard

He took it to the twenty-four-hour Kinko's across from the apartment complex. Even after midnight it wasn't easy crossing the street on foot. One carload of kids in an old Plymouth Fury were so amused to see a man actually trying to cross the six lanes of Fort Pierce Boulevard that they whooped and honked and reached their hands out and pounded the car doors as they roared past.

After the envelopes were filled and addressed and stamped and sealed, Bob stood out on the balcony and watched the traffic and listened to the dry tire sound from all directions. After all the phone calls and the hours of carrying boxes down to the car, back and forth between the chill of the apartment and the blanket of heat outside, with his shirt soaked through, this was the first time in three days he'd had a chance just to stand out here and think about Roy being dead and not have to do something about it. The television was already packed in the back of the car, along with books and comedy records, so much weight pressing down the back of the station wagon that when Bob had tried to drive the car at night, people kept blinking their lights even though he had his low beams on.

The only thing he had forgotten to do was clean up all the cigarette butts that were lying out here on the concrete balcony. Maybe the last cigarette Roy ever smoked was out here, when he already knew he was going into the hospital—but no, Bob remembered, he was still smoking even in the hospital. At that point it didn't matter. He was so doped up that the cigarette kept falling out of his mouth, and Bob had to help him scramble after it in the rumpled bedsheets, while the voices of defense lawyers droned from a tiny color TV at the end of a long jointed arm connected to the same bedside console where the buttons to call the nurse were located.

What does a man know about his brother? When Bob left the hospital that night to go back to the apartment, Roy looked at him and said, "Thanks." Bob thought he just meant thanks for finding the cigarette. But the phone in the apartment was already ringing by the time he got the door open, and Roy was dead.

People think about weird things. As Bob drove back to the hospital that night, the only thing he could bring himself to think about was television, a business that he was thinking more and more he should have stayed with for a few more years at least, instead of ending up as a not quite old man talking shop to himself in traffic on the way to say good-bye to someone who would not be able to hear him because he was dead.

The main thing Bob couldn't stop thinking about, there in Roy's loose-springed car, was that Roy had been watching the same trial on his little television for twelve hours a day, and it was still only half over. In all his years in the syndication business, cataloging and summarizing episodes of *The Dick Van Dyke Show* and *Adam 12* for little stations that couldn't afford to buy the whole run, Bob had learned how important it is for a story always to have a beginning and an end, and that the upshot of a story, even *My Favorite Martian,* always has to affirm that we live in an orderly universe, where the vast majority of people are basically decent, where school bullies are reduced to tears in front of the class, and criminals, as if to affirm how hopeless it is to be a criminal in the first place, will try to escape in the last ten minutes by climbing up tall construction scaffolds that have been already surrounded by the police. An old human instinct, maybe, to climb a tree and hope the lion will get tired of waiting and go away. And now Roy was cheated out of his right to see the end of the story, to see that two thousand dollar suit led away for the last time, all the heavy television watchers waving good-bye from their Barcaloungers.

* * *

The Oldsmobile lost its power steering on I-95 in South Carolina, next to a billboard for a giant tourist and truck stop complex called South of the Border, in which a little figure named Pedro, whose head and sombrero extended a few feet above the main part of the sign, was saying "SEÑOR WANTS A COLD DREENK, I THEENK."

Bob drove along the shoulder at twenty miles an hour as the front end screeched and smoked, and tractor trailers, streamlined with plastic fairings, slammed past, jolting the Oldsmobile in a wave of displaced air.

From the South of the Border Service Center, he called the number on Roy's Keystone Motor Club booklet to see if they would reimburse him for the tow and got a girl on the line who spoke with a New York accent so rich and zaftig that Bob remembered all at once how long he'd been away from the real world and how much he wanted to get that car moving north again.

Bob had always wondered what it is about being retired that pulls so many people south—maybe the same gravity that pulls the flesh of their faces down—into the heat and the flatness and the kids cruising around in boom-boom cars and the towns that blend into each other with nothing to mark the beginning of one and the end of another except a new name on the side of another windowless bank building. Dorothy talked about it sometimes, feeling him out on the subject, but whatever that geographical force was that affected everybody else so strongly, it hadn't gotten him yet.

Each pay phone in this row of carrels opposite the fuel desk had in front of it a full ashtray the size of a cereal bowl. A yellow sheet of paper taped in each carrel announced RETURN LOADS AVAILABLE TO THE WEST COAST. To his right a picture window overlooked one end of the parking lot, where Bob could see a trailer with steps leading up to a door in the side of it and a sign above the door announcing FAMILY MINISTRIES OF THE OPEN ROAD.

Beside the center window, which looked out to where the big slope-nosed trucks were fueling up, Bob could see an entire rotating rack of bumper stickers for sale, saying things like CLINTON DOESN'T INHALE—HE SUCKS! and HONK IF YOU ALREADY KNOW WHO MURDERED VINCE FOSTER.

* * *

All day the hiss of air-conditioning came down from a register in the ceiling beside the bathroom door. Roy's ashes rested next to the "Pedro's Hints for Guests" folder on the counter that ran the length of the motel room, across from the two double beds. The ashes had come in a box much bigger than Bob expected, about half the size of a shoe box, wrapped in brown paper, bearing a label with Roy's name typed below the "Memorial Concepts" logo.

It wasn't a bad room, for South of the Border. Out of curiosity he bought *TV Guide* in the convenience store and found out about a local show called *Little Audrey and Friends*, with some of the same King Features shorts that his company had done so well reselling when nobody else in the business was interested.

He walked around the whole South of the Border complex, from the reptile display to Pedro's Cantina to Senor Bang-Bang's Fireworks Supermarket, where men and boys dressed identically in shorts and T-shirts hurried in and hurried out, with the gaudy shapes and colors of explosives protruding from the tops of brown shopping bags.

He wandered through the truck stop parking lot, surrounded by the gargling roar of hundreds of idling diesel engines, an incredible sound, spreading out for a hundred acres, the earth alive. One of the companies, a big fleet called Covenant Transport, carried the same antiabortion message on the rear of every trailer. Bob wondered briefly what would happen if any driver ever dared to say anything about carrying a placard he might not agree with, but with all the combustion noise around, the thought didn't last very long. Never had Bob had such a clear understanding of all the things meant and implied by the term *non-union*.

The car came back so late Thursday afternoon that he'd already checked in for another night. He walked around some more and went swimming while the pool wasn't yet busy and there were still only a few families checked in for the night, only a few kids thumping along the concrete on their heels, the way kids always walk in bare feet around a pool.

At least it was good to hear real kids around. The motel before this one had been in Florence, South Carolina, which is apparently the place where people all over the South come for cheap dentures and bridgework. The sign in front of his Comfort Inn had said "WELCOME DENTAL PATIENTS." An entire vending machine in the lobby sold nothing but painkillers: aspirin, buffered aspirin, acetaminophen, ibuprofen, methyl salicylate.

* * *

Even through the careful wrapping of brown paper, the ashes had started to give off a strange smell, hard and scratchy, like the upper notes of somebody's bad breath—unless it was the car, maybe an ashtray in back that he'd forgotten to clean out. It was the Forth of July. He drove and drove in the thick traffic, on three lanes of pavement that seemed to get whiter and whiter as the day got hotter and hotter.

What poem is that line from: "a little boy thinking long thoughts"? He'd read it somewhere, but he couldn't remember where. Now he was thinking his own long thoughts, thoughts about as far as you could get from whatever that poem was actually supposed to be about, as he sat there, driving, with nothing else to do, the easiest job in the world, in the continuous machine of traffic, across a field of tiny tobacco seedlings, through the cooked pulpy sweetness of a paper mill town.

Long thoughts. You can think one thought for the whole time it takes to get from the top of one rise to the top of the next and another thought starting from the point where you first see the McDonald's arches on a pole hundreds of feet high and ending at the moment you get to it. What you learn from driving all day is that the longer you can think about something, the simpler it becomes. Really two thoughts, over and over, touch each other at different angles: What it's like to be alive, in a car, bored, tired—or in the hospital, trying to say thanks when there's so much poison in your blood that your face is a deep yellow and your brother doesn't know if you mean thanks for finding the cigarette or thanks for being my brother. And then what it's like, or more accurately what it's not like, to be a bunch of stuff in a little box in the backseat for Jim and Rich to scatter in the surf at Wildwood, New Jersey, unless that's not legal anymore.

Thinking. Soon it began to get dark, and up ahead he saw the bursts of a municipal fireworks display starting. He watched it as he passed, the perfect spheres blooming in the late dusk, and a few miles later some more going off. Something about the South is so friendly, even through car windows, that it doesn't matter that all the rotten things you know about it are true. To drive through those states is like visiting an entire nation where nobody ever gets cancer. It was nice to be able to see the fireworks shows one after another, sometimes the displays from two different towns at the same time, the far off Christmas bulb colors flashing over the black horizon of trees.

This was always Roy's favorite holiday. He and the boys would drive down to Delaware and come back with whole hundred dollar assortments of rockets and flowerpots and buzz bombs and Roman candles and Black Cats and lady fingers, all those dense and bright paper colors and shapes spread out on the porch under a floodlight. His kids always had cherry bombs and M-80s to set off under coffee cans, made in the old short Maxwell House shape that they don't sell anymore, sending them high up into the trees in front of a house.

Bob passed a Howard Johnson lodge with a Vacancy sign. He could have pulled in, but some fireworks were still going off in the distance, and he still had some more things to keep thinking about. You get tired in a car, but it's just as much work to stop as it is not to, so you go on, watching, driving, thinking. He was going to have to remember to wrap the ashes in a plastic bag if the smell got any worse, if that's where it was actually coming from.

He noticed for the first time that those bursts are prettier from far away, when you can't hear anybody saying "oooh" and "aaah," but you can see the spheres and the colors, and you don't have to think about how many hours of television those families are watching on the nights when there aren't any fireworks or what sort of things they are teaching their kids about angels during the designated half hour of every night when the television is supposed to be off.

He had planned to find a motel an hour ago, just to be sure he didn't get stuck with a hundred miles of No Vacancy signs, but for now the car was humming, those circles of lights were bursting out of nothing in the darkness, and he didn't have to go to the bathroom, so he figured he'd just go and go and take a chance on a motel somewhere an hour or so to the north after the firework displays had gone dark and everybody was back home watching television.

hot plate

Cabrito al carbón. Salsa roja. Blosser is thinking in Spanish, though he doesn't really know how to speak it, except for a few restaurant-related phrases, thinking as he always does on his last call of the day, even filling in on the blackboard at the back of his eyes those rolling diacritical squiggles that English doesn't have a name for. From speakers bracketed in the crooks where walls meet ceiling, the music of Autoharp and hammer dulcimer fills the store with stringy, woodstove, old lady trills. Jasmine incense drifts between the racks of hanging knitwear. *Legumbres verdes. Hígado con huevos.*

The store manager twirls a handful of lusterless brown hair as she pages through the plastic loose-leaf windows of the catalog. Blosser reads the familiar captions upside down, his sister Sandy's precise calligraphy, the color prints of Sandy's sweaters and knit dresses lined up across the middle of each page ... like specials clipped onto the middle of a menu, is what he's thinking. Wednesday: *Pescados gordos*. Thursday: *Refritos Monterrey*.

To say that Blosser is hungry for Mexican food at this time of the afternoon is the same as saying that the sun is getting lower in the sky. Its nearly horizontal yellow reflects off a college town full of Japanese cars. Students pass on all sides of his leased Cressida, most hunched down a little too dramatically into their yellow and black parkas, hurrying to dormitory dining halls, to McDonald's, or to bleached-smelling, mucus-free, animal rights kitchens.

Blosser knows that the college girls walking to supper in bright synthetics would pay more attention to him if he were driving one of those uncircumcised-looking two-seat stud cars with its name skewed toward the last letters of the alphabet, such as most kids in college have to work full-time to pay the insurance on. But he needs room for samples and last-minute deliveries, so he has settled for this spiritless Japanese four-door, designed, he imagines, for middle-aged women who are selling real estate to American families so dazed by everything around them being Japanese that they could not locate the city of Detroit on a map if you gave them a hundred pin-the-tail-on-the-donkey stickers.

That's something you have to understand if you want to do business in college towns (though he's not complaining): All non-BMW cars must be Japanese. If Blosser pulled up in a Ford Taurus, he wouldn't fit in at all in towns like this; people would think he was presidential candidate Pat Buchanan looking for the yeshiva school crosswalk and a chance to chalk another one up on his fuselage. In ritzier towns, a Lexus would sound the right note. But here, where a good percentage of the educated people still believe in multiple, overlapping conspiracy theories, Blosser knows that a man in a Toyota will be taken seriously.

Dinner, with paperwork not exactly caught up, but close enough. Now, the moment of truth. Or not. This is Wisconsin, after all. In the Days Inn phone book, thin as a restaurant menu, he has found the most likely place: Los Pepinos, the name bordered by a simple square, with none of that red printing that's supposed to make the chili peppers look hotter, no border work of guitars and saguaros.

A promising graphic, he thinks, as the traffic thins toward the opposite end of town from his motel. Blosser's mind, on schedule, becomes a kitchen full of beefy steam rolling across the ceiling from a range top full of fried peppers lanced open, the little flat seeds trembling in the juice, giving off a caustic vapor so hot that just thinking about it can make him bounce up and down in the driver's seat—not dramatically enough for people in the other cars to see him. He thinks about the Spanish voices that echo over the clang of pots and dishes, over the cracked music of a kitchen radio, where a waiter in a hurry shouts through the arch where the order slips flutter in the warm breeze on their alligator clips: *Bistec a la peligrosa! Frijoles con broma! Brazos del perro pasado por viento!* Some dream, in Wisconsin. He knows he will be lucky if he gets a waitress who can say "*Sí señor.*"

* * *

"The condition is called *Thermophiliosis culinaris*, and it strikes one out of every 250 million Americans." That's what he says to himself most nights, on the way to someplace where both the Spanish guitar music and the enchiladas will probably turn out to be so bland that, as he drives away, he will not be able to remember whether he rinsed his mouth out in the men's room.

T.C., as he calls it, is a disease that will follow you around this country like a tin can on a dog's tail. To be what he is, a culinary thermophile, to lust in the direction of those occasional cantinas that dare to put even a little fire in their chimichangas, is like being the unluckiest gambler in the world. Every day sizzles with promise; every night is a plunge into cold dishwater.

But even the worst gambler knows that one day the cold structures around you have to open and let you through for just a moment, at least let you see into that lost restaurant-scape you have been dreaming about—a world of steaming kitchens, a table with chipped glassware, and once every few years, those tiny and ferocious yellow peppers lying at the side of your plate like minnows.

It happened in Saint Cloud, Minnesota, of all places, in a place converted from a Wendy's, with colored cellophane glued on the windows for stained glass and on the radio a long retrospective called "Motown Memories." He had a good visit one night when he was staying in Jefferson City, Missouri; the kitchen was directly under the glide path of the airport and from its front entrance he could smell the oven exhaust from the restaurant next door, the rustic but pricey Scotch 'n' Stroganoff.

This is life on the road, or at least the part of Blosser's life that comes with enough problems to give him something to lie awake worrying about, trying to decide if he should get up and drape some towels over the very bright digital time numerals on the motel television. The work part of Blosser's life is easy, as long as he keeps the sales and shipping records straight, with Sandy's catalog to show people and the sample sweaters that she makes specially for him to wear on his calls.

Not much social life in this business. His wife, Janine, has gone the way of a salesman's wife—as people on the road talk about—gone amicably, uncontested, into a friendship that consists mainly of long, handwritten Christmas cards.

You don't meet people in hotel bars anymore, not even drunks. Everybody is too busy watching basketball. The phone books in some of the bigger towns have listings for services like "Cadillac Companions," and he's called them a few times, but the girls tend to be a little brusque. They get suspicious of Blosser's beefy face and his good teeth, and they take such a long time checking him out, looking through his wallet and asking him what his mother's maiden name is, that even after they decide he's okay, they still conduct the rest of the session with a sort of lingering resentment over his having *almost* been a cop.

He misses Los Pepinos on his first pass, sees the building numbers growing past 1720, then turns around in the parking lot of the Family Security Bank. It's a good sign when a restaurant is small enough and homely enough that you miss it the first time. Another good sign: no floodlights in the parking lot. Bad sign: They take American Express. Good sign: a wooden front door that squeaks against its frame. Bad sign: a hostess whose job it is to do nothing but seat people.

The first thing he notices as he follows the girl to the non-smoking section is that there is a distinct absence of embroidered velvet sombreros on the walls. Velvet sombreros, of course, are one of the worst possible signs; they are acceptable only in those many restaurants that are actually named *El Sombrero*. (In Kenosha, Wisconsin, where the non-Spanish-speaking management understands neither grammatical gender nor seasoning, it is called *La* Sombrero.)

He has opened one of those big, shiny Howard Johnson–type menus (wrong), with a separate page of hot dogs and fried chicken for the Gringos, a page for the *Niños*, and a page of "heart smart" portions for the not very well translated Padre-Grandes. The flow of his digestive juices, already stanched by the Denny's-like lamination of the menu, squeezes down to nothing when he becomes aware of the worst sign of all, standing above him: a blonde waitress who speaks perfect English.

"I'm sorry," she says with that rubbery embarrassed smile he knows so well. "We only have Corona."

If Blosser had any guts—other than the one pressing against the edge of his table—he'd grab his sweater, make an excuse about having forgotten to meet somebody, and get out. A Mexican restaurant that rejects Tecate in favor of that ultimate college student beer might as well move to the space next to the entranceway of the mall and get rich off the Saturday shopping family crowd. A Mexican restaurant without Tecate might as well put green food coloring in its beer for St. Patrick's Day and then serve it so cold even American beer would taste good.

But then he is not being fair to American beer. After all, everybody must remember one American beer that tasted genuinely good for the duration of one strictly demarked period in one's life. If you keep on drinking it, you are living in the past. There was a time—the same summer in Colorado when he met Connie and she took him to bed and turned her back to him and then turned him into a thermophile—when a can of Budweiser tasted as brave and bright as the red and white lettering on the can, a time when Blosser had mastered the trick of being able to drink one so fast that he could finish it before the heat-conducting aluminum had raised the remaining beer to body temperature.

* * *

Things in this dining room are beginning to look a little too much like Wisconsin. Blosser has always treasured pretty waitresses anyplace but in a Mexican restaurant. Any businessman who works on the road knows that the continued existence of beautiful waitresses is the only sign we have left that at least God has not given up, even if the rest of us have. Unfortunately, the beautiful waitresses at Los Pepinos are also a good sign that God prefers to order from the Gringos page.

Worse and worse: The toilet is as clean as his bathroom back at the Days Inn. He remembers a place that Connie took him, the weekend they drove to Santa Fe, where you had to go outside in a sort of plywood stall, with chickens crowing and flapping next door. None of that "employees must wash their hands" stuff. In the kitchen of that place there was so much pepper in the steam of the air that you didn't need to wash your hands; cholera germs would have perished like a moth in a gas flame.

The designers of Los Pepinos have set the booths around the edges of the dining room, lining them up into a series of arched cloisters. The framed watercolors on the stucco walls are quite good—tasteful renderings of mustard-colored adobe missions.

A real place would have paintings on black velvet. In fact, a Mexican restaurant is the only place where black velvet art is a good sign, and the most dedicated pilgrims hope, as they walk in the door, that the furniture will look like something from an old mobile home.

* * *

Blosser used to bring his own Tabasco and crushed red pepper and ground cayenne and chili powder and cumin, a little pharmacopoeia that he carried in a miniature Band-Aid box in the inside pocket of one of his cardigans, to be prepared for those occasions when the chef had never been to Mexico. But he doesn't carry those flavorings anymore. People who could see him through the arch of his cloistered stall would look at him funny. Waitresses thought he was trying to embarrass the management. And if he tried adding the spices surreptitiously, he felt like one of those people you see at water fountains trying to be discreet about taking their medication, throwing back their head slowly, as if they're really just interested in something they've noticed on the ceiling.

There was another problem with the flavor canisters: They didn't work. The hotness in Mexican food lives down deep, like the heat inside volcanic rocks. You just look at those rocks on PBS, hardened at the edge of a crocodile-shaped lava flow, and you can tell how hot they are. That's what Mexican food is, on the rare occasions when it's right. It's like the distortion in an electric guitar. Once you hear one song played that way, everything else for the rest of your life will sound like skating rink music.

The spices coming from outside, after the fact, never quite work. If you find yourself in a mild-flavored establishment, you can try to make yourself believe you're eating some heat. You can pour on so much Tabasco and red pepper that you have to tamp the taste down with a flour tortilla from that slippery plastic canister they come in, and you can wash it all down with whatever limeless, super-chilled fraternity slosh they have charged you four dollars for, but inevitably you will discover the dead interior of each mouthful, like the rubbery underside of chicken. At that moment, the Aztec-derived orange-and-brown geometric print of the tabletop will go as gray as the snow melting in the parking lot. The food will lie still in your mouth. Nothing will happen. You will forget everything you have tasted by the time you get halfway to the bathroom. And you will know where you are: the land of family dining. Nothing wrong with it, really, except for being horrible. Baby bibs, embroidered with iridescent green saguaros, hang beside each cloister.

* * *

Sometimes the summer when a man learns what he is going to spend his life caring about is so big that all he can do is quit school and not go back, as a sort of tribute to how much of a time it was and how much of a person he was in the middle of it. This is always a good thing to think about when you are waiting for the waitress to bring your chips and salsa. How he and Connie ended up together, among the shapeless mash of people moving in and out of the cheap rooming house that used to be the Sandstone Palace Hotel, he never figured out. All he knew was that in the days after they both lost their jobs at the same resort hotel at the very beginning of the summer, she used to come into his room and hang around whenever her roommate had somebody over.

Connie was almost as tall as he was, a swimming instructor with an occasional ice cream problem. She liked to sit on his bed and stretch her tanned legs across his while she spooned Rocky Road directly from the carton.

On the Fourth of July weekend, along with Connie's roommate and the roommate's boyfriend, they took a trip down to New Mexico in Blosser's Volkswagen. Every restaurant Connie picked out for them was a Mexican place with Formica tables and steam from the kitchen fogging the windows. No air-conditioning in the Volkswagen, but they didn't miss it. At that time in your life, you didn't think about air-conditioning; you just drove along at seventy-five miles an hour, perfectly happy in a glaze of sweat, with the air slamming against your ears.

Blosser still has a photograph of Connie, leaning against the fender of his black Beetle. It's not a very good picture. She looks glum and hangdog behind aviator sunglasses with her mouth half open and her short hair slick with sweat against the freckles of her forehead. In the background you can see the adobe fronts of the shops and offices of Taos and the fake ends of the supporting beams sticking out into the sun.

It was so hot that day that you can see it in the picture. Everything seems to exist in a gray fog, a secret fact of heat that blankets the angle-parked American cars under something thick and invisible and so real that for the rest of Blosser's life, when he looks at those blurred dummy beams sticking out above the Rosita Waters Gallery, he will remember, as clearly as he remembers how the green sauce tastes when you crush a seed between your teeth, how hot that day was.

At night, when they spread the sleeping bags tentless around the car, Connie wouldn't let him touch her, though just a few feet away her roommate panted and shrieked. The moon was so bright that he couldn't keep from watching.

And all that weekend, food. Connie refused to stop at a single non-Mexican place. You could lift a forkful of meat, and when you put it in your mouth, it would be alive in a way food east of the Mississippi never was, something radiating in all directions into your throat and sinuses. You eat one of those tiny peppers on the side of the plate, a Mexican equivalent of the forlorn pickle slice beside a hamburger, and it becomes part of your life. Ten miles down the road, twenty miles, the inside of your head will be alive with it as you inhale the Volkswagen's heated air against the evaporative cooler of your tongue.

* * *

"Here you are, sir," the blonde waitress says, prim in the Castilian ruffles of her blouse, as she sets down the salsa and chips. He crunches. They are Doritos. He dips. It is Ortega.

There is a kind of dizzy and abandoned pleasure to the moment when you realize all is lost. He wishes he could be sensitive enough to wipe away a tear at a time like this, but the only tears Blosser cares about are the kind that will not happen tonight, the kind of tears he gets when a yellow pepper catches him by surprise.

All around, from speakers concealed in the ceiling beams, the instrumental music plays, mariachi-style, authentic-sounding, but a little too clean. A real mariachi band needs one drunk, that suppressed squawk of an off-key trumpet, giving its own kind of heat within the notes, a kind of scratch in the texture, if for no other purpose than to keep the needle from slipping off the record.

* * *

When they got back to Colorado, Connie was strange. Her kitten peed on the bed, and she threw it against the wall and it died—or at least it died and that's how he reconstructed it. She knocked on his door in the middle of the night and said she had tried to kill herself with sleeping pills.

Blosser walked her around and around the block, the only remedy he knew, which he'd seen in one of Dr. Hippocrates's articles, from the front of the Sandstone to the Jenny Lind Coffee Shop to the Onion Slice (whose vented steak vapor used to blow into Blosser's window while he was making peanut butter sandwiches), around and around, until the street-cleaning truck came on duty with its flashing blue light, and Blosser's knees ached from walking, and she still wouldn't talk to him.

The night she finally brought him to bed, she had taken some bad acid. Her skin was like ash as she lay on her back, her head turned away from him, all the swimmer's suppleness gone from her body. Every time he put his arm around her, she pulled away.

"When you touch my breast," she said, "I see a thousand breasts."

* * *

The main course hasn't come and already Blosser is miserable. There's just so much in these restaurants that you can take. If only there was some way to make it legal again to have some form of constitutionally permissible segregation, in which all the little mommy-baby families in their minivans could be restricted to one class of restaurant, goo-gooing over the gentle enchilada filling, with Blosser welcome everywhere else for a meal that he can remember all the way back to his motel. All the way back to the basketball game.

* * *

Connie was very honest about it, at least. She told him she had needed a warm body that night to keep the hallucinations away. They stayed friends for his last weeks there, though it was hard to look at her without thinking of her seeing a thousand breasts.

It occurred to Blosser that this wasn't just the least romantic thing she had ever said to him; it was the least romantic thing any person or any creature had ever uttered in the history of sexual dimorphism.

He remembers taking her to dinner just before he started the trip home, how the simulated torchlight of Los Papagallos, flicking back and forth between twin filaments, softened her face, made a blur across her skin, her brown, toughening outdoor skin that he knows by now is probably crazed with tiny sun wrinkles, or worse.

They hooked arms for tequila shots. In those days, it was perfectly normal for everybody to start a trip drunk and then drive all night, sobering up. When he kissed her good-bye that night, both of them leaning against the packed Bug, he could feel on her lips the graininess of salt, the best kiss she ever gave him, to tell the truth, and he could taste the lingering heat of *chorizos rojos*.

It was years ago, in a basin by the mountains, in a town so small that nobody could believe how brown the air got when the sun started breaking the molecules apart. It would be nice to think a man could leave that town in the middle of the night and thereafter be frozen in time, with his Budweiser and the memory of salt on a girl's lips—the great thermophile, the cruelly tormented thermophile who must have said the wrong thing, back in the sixties, told somebody carrying a package to hurry up, and is condemned now to range forever across the snowy flats of Toyota-land.

It comes to his table with as much ceremony as a birthday cake.

"Watch the plate," she says. "It's *reeeeeeeeally hot!*"

* * *

Driving back to the motel he starts having thoughts of the kind he can tolerate only on a full stomach: He didn't hate it. He hasn't hated it for years; that's the problem, when you get right down to it. These nights have been shaping up the same way for a long time: He starts out angry, but he can't keep it going.

The rich crumb breading that clings to the *chiles rellenos* was mild, let's face it. So was the filling inside. It will not make a man jump up and down nor cause him to whack his arm against one side of his chest and go "Nik! Nik!" like Jack Nicholson in *Easy Rider* when he takes his first drink of the morning.

It will not wake a man up in the middle of the night with thoughts of Connie hallucinating a thousand breasts, Connie with zinc oxide on her nose, throwing her head back to swallow the mezcal worm, or worse: Connie coming home from the dermatologist, pale with the bad news.

It wasn't bad. He liked it. Even the Doritos. Tomorrow he will be strong enough to hate it again; he already knows that the restaurants in Duluth are so gentle he will have a good opportunity to grind his teeth over the mild quesadillas.

He lies in bed with his contacts out, his teeth brushed and flossed, no interdental trace of anything he's tasted all day. His life stretches out in all directions, as cool and wide as a king-size bed. He touches the remote control, fixed to the side table like a little artillery piece. He flicks and flicks until finally the basketball men appear, blurring back and forth in their bright singlets with the sound off.

a puddle of sex books

How it starts is that a man is driving in the desert and a woman passes him in a car, and she is naked. Then there is something about how she pulls in for gas and somebody else sees her, maybe an old man. Or maybe by then she's curled up in the backseat of somebody else's car. The sight of her bare breasts revives some long-buried stirrings in the old gas station attendant, or words to that effect.

All he knew was that the story took place in spring, in the desert. George read it page by waterlogged page, surrounded by mud and water in the half dimness of trees out in back of his house, sitting on the friendly rock he and his friends had named Roger. Whatever details were missing from the story—sex organs, penetration, bodily fluids—he wouldn't have noticed. At fourteen, or whatever age, in the spring, in the middle of the wet dirt, he wouldn't have known the difference between soft-core and hard-core. He would not have remembered whether the story was told by the first guy driving who saw her; it was only later that he realized that, except for the letters column in *Penthouse,* you don't see much pornography narrated in the first person.

Somehow the man and the woman get together in the desert at the gas station, and they drive around and perform the sex act over and over again without penises or vaginas, just breasts all over the place, bursting out from her skimpy underwear and the two naked, or partially naked, bodies clutching and climbing over each other, nonpenetratively, the way George used to do with his sister's Barbie and Ken dolls.

The only title George remembered was *Sex Bomb,* but there were several of the books, all soaked from where he found them, in a pool of water at the edge of the woods somewhere. He stuffed them into the imitation leather saddlebag of his three-speed Rudge. Where they came from he never figured out. Maybe somebody felt guilty. Maybe somebody's mother found them, or somebody needed to throw them away and didn't want the garbage collectors to see them.

George read the first of the books out in the woods, in a clear patch out in the half dark, where sometimes when it was wet enough they used to find strings of frog's eggs. The whole book was so wet he had to tear the pages off as he went and throw them, soft as leaves, on the ground.

The man and the woman had the sex act again and again, driving around. On a cliff, in the bushes. Then what? They had some kind of a bad fight, with only a few soaked pages left to be torn off and the rest in a pile beside the rock. The ground was so soft in those days that you didn't have to bury anything; you could just kick it underneath the duff of leaves, and the top layer would fold over like rubber and let your foot in. The only thing George remembers from the end of the book is that they have such a bad fight that the man punches her in the breast, and then somebody else dies, male or female he didn't know, and the car goes over the cliff, with somebody in it screaming, and that was the end, a pile of wet pages to be jammed into the ground, the same soaked smell as the leaves and the water.

For years afterward, the scene where the man punches her in the breast made him wince, like remembering the time he was playing softball with his sister Karen in the field down the long driveway from their house, just the two of them. She bounced a bad underhand pitch in front of him, which he shouldn't have reached down and swung at, but he golfed it on the bounce straight at her and hit her in the breast.

She must have been old enough for it to be a real breast. He couldn't get her to stop crying. She was still crying as they rode their bicycles back up the driveway, both of them standing up on the pedals, the bikes tilting beneath them from side to side, Karen still crying and George still saying "I'm sorry, I'm sorry."

It was terrible for that man to punch her breast like that at the end of a book where people are supposed to be nice to each other so men can masturbate. Anybody knows that a punch was made for a cowboy's face and nothing else. Once in a family crisis, George punched the dog in the face, and that was terrible too. It made a sound almost like the sound on television. His father never said anything about it, but George could feel it for years.

It's not fair that George's sister had to cry and cry and heft her Royce Gazelle up the hill, and it's not fair that some fictional nice girl with big breasts, an explosive sexual appetite, and no functioning genitals should have to go over a cliff like that—if that's who it was in the car—it spoils the story. There were so many places remaining out there in the little excited narrative universe where she could have performed the sex act and maybe awakened buried stirrings in some other old men watching through a crack in a tin storage shed.

And maybe it's not fair that the guy who wrote it was such a sad old drudge for a penny a word that he didn't know any better. By now he's probably as dead as the rats sniffing around a drainpipe in an old Nazi movie. Or if he's not dead, maybe he's stupid, reads nothing, listens to talk radio in traffic, loud, has never even heard of the famous novel where that woman gets down under the covers and does something so cruel (though justified in context) to her abusive boyfriend or husband that male graduate students who were required to read it are vague about the other chapters, but they still wince when they think about that scene.

The weird thing about the past is that if you want to get seriously involved with it, you have to be a mathematician. You have to keep a chart showing who did what and who deserves what. One mistake will throw the whole equation out of trim; the author who got tenure the day that book was published will be found to have sneaked some lines in that nobody knew about, with the result that when her name comes up over a microphone, the people who no longer clap will be ashamed of the ones who still do.

Once, on television, in subtitles, a Japanese girl said, "The ground is warm under my feet." This was years later, when George was trying to learn Japanese, and for the first time he understood something about those days when he rode around with the books soaking in his saddlebag; it was just as interesting when nothing happened as when something happened. There is a corner in one of the subdivisions where there is no traffic, and kids have been riding bicycles around in a circle for so long that the kids riding now weren't even born when George and his friends were there. They always go counterclockwise. It is in the nature of the Northern Hemisphere that you will never see them ride clockwise. His father took the bike in to have the chain tightened, and George forgot about the books, and the bicycle mechanic found them.

"Too hot to handle," was the mechanic's joke. The whole cloth side of the imitation leather was rotten, so the whole pouch had to come off, and everything got thrown away. A lean look now to the bicycle, with the seat high and nothing under it. The road was warm under his tires. They were a good family. They teased him a little about the books, but nobody made a big deal about it.

It was true about the ground. You could scratch your finger into it and feel the warmth from inside. Your finger would come up brown as fertilizer but clean, with no grains under your fingernail.

Things went back into the ground or else they came out of it and got their heads cut off. Mrs. Burns, who lived across the street from the end of the long driveway, had hired a man with a tractor to mow the field across from the entrance to George's driveway. The sickle bar had cut through a nest of rabbits. Karen came running, crying, around to the back of the house where George was digging with a stainless steel spoon against the side of the poured concrete foundation. Their friend Oliver Stanton from next door was running behind her.

"It's *murder*!" they were both shouting. Oliver deserves to be credited as the one who originally invented the game of "Booties." George was the oldest one, so they came to him, which was nice, but there was nothing he could do. It was just some old man with a tractor and the jiggling squeak of the sickle bar. As they ran across the flattened rows of the cut field, which George would learn in poetry class should rightly be called a *swale,* they could see the cut rabbits from a long way off, a mild red, almost orange under the green.

"Booties" is a game played with a cat, in which you tear a section of paper towel into four squares and with a rubber band attach a square, like a little bag, over each of the cat's feet and watch the cat trudge, or dance. Every cat does it differently. Most people said it was cruel. Perhaps George was the only person who knew the difference between being mean and being cruel; he knew that if you loved your cat, you could be mean without being cruel.

A woman from two houses down called the police and said George's family was living with their chickens. Every night the fire siren went off, and sometimes George thought it was the end of the world, but then when it wasn't it somehow didn't register, and two nights later he thought the same thing. One night he dreamed it was the end of the world and his father and Khrushchev were lying on the roof, laughing.

Oliver and George and Karen and Oliver's two brothers went for ice cream, under the yellow lights, on the nights they could get Oliver's father to drive them down there, to a town at the edge of a trailer park, where the main highway ran so close to the swamp that every streetlight was a blizzard of bugs. It must have been longer ago than he thought; the first time he ever saw an electric guitar was in the doorway of the Gulf station, two fat boys on stools playing minor chords, the moisture from the swamp blowing in across the Gulftane pumps.

George and Karen used to go out behind the house into their father's garden and eat raspberries. It must have rained all the time, but George can't remember it. The garden grew like a jungle. Karen had the "Old King Cole" dream. A big fat man was spanking her with a board with a nail in it, and she was laughing. Daffy Duck was strapped into the electric chair, in the garden, laughing in that *whoo-whoo* way, until the current slammed his face shut.

It must have been April Fool's Day. They put worms in the refrigerator. Up the road, where the bad kids lived, a dog was sick. Some kid had a .22, so they decided to shoot him. He went stiff, convulsed. Somewhere on the same road, Oliver Stanton was playing with some of the other bad kids who were burning .22 bullets in a fire. He didn't tell George this until a year later. One of the bullets went off crooked, and the slug skinned the side of Oliver's head. In trouble. The heaviness of those words, like the heaviness of dirt locked under the ground, under the rubbery duff of leaves. The kids from up the road walked with him, pleading with him not to tell. There was something sad about that pleading. These were the bad kids, but now they were almost crying, because they knew how much trouble they were in. Oliver Stanton was a real gentleman. He told his mother he fell on a rock, even though she was a registered nurse and must have known he was lying.

Every few months Karen would show up in the kitchen, silent at first, her face collapsed, meaning the cat had been run over. She must have known the cats were going to get run over, but when they did she cried just as hard as ever, like the time she went down the driveway to play softball with George again and got hit in the breast a second time. Unless George is remembering the same thing twice, the two of them once more on their bicycles zigzagging heavily up the hill and her crying—like that poor naked woman in the car having to go through the sex act over and over again so some old guy reading the book could get excited about how big her breasts were.

After a while he had thought about these things so many times that he didn't even know if the next thing happened at all. But if he hit the ball, and he hit the dog, maybe he did this too. The cat disappeared just before she had kittens. A week later he found the cat, twenty yards downhill from the road, lying on her back, her belly soft and fat as a Buddha, bloated, spread, almost flat, liquid inside. She had already started to sink back into the wet ground.

George doesn't remember whether he made it a joke and led Karen down the hill for a surprise, or told her in good faith, or planned it as a joke and thought better of it halfway up the driveway or halfway back down. What is remarkable is that she wasn't angry. She just stood there in the tall grass looking down at the rot, and her face collapsed. Again, afterward, they rode together up the hill, the Rudge and the Gazelle, straining against their pedals, the sound of her crying absorbed by the thick green in every direction. They rode uphill past the little cement-block house that Vernon Short and his wife were renting from George and Karen's parents, who had been recommended to them through the church as somebody who wouldn't discriminate against them for being a racially mixed couple—unless this was at a time when they hadn't moved in yet or had already left.

It was a long driveway, and she cried all the way up, pedaling. She carefully set the kickstand before she ran into the house to cry some more. Strange how the sound of that crying went through the house, room to room and year to year, from the time the chair caught on fire to all the times over breakfast with another cat run over and her face hanging, collapsed. If she had ever stopped crying, that house would have been dead. She cried when war broke out in Africa. She cried for four hours when she couldn't see *Darby O'Gill and the Little People*.

They went to see *Old Yeller*, and it was weird, because at the end of the movie, when Old Yeller was dead, all the kids were crying, and then instead of turning up the houselights, they played a cartoon. It was the one where Donald Duck and Huey, Dewey, and Louie are sledding, and every time the nephews build a snowman, Donald Duck smashes through it with his sled and laughs that cruel, choking, convulsive laugh. Then he aims the sled at another snowman, a squat, bulky-shaped construction—but this one his nephews have built around a boulder. The sled splinters, and the metal runners get wrapped around Donald's beak, and his nephews fall all over each other and slap themselves and laugh in that same constricted, genetically determined way. The weirdest thing was that all the kids in the theater were laughing for a few minutes, but when the cartoon was over, they were all crying again.

George had a dream that something was wrong with the moon. A sled caught fire in the snow. Karen had the same dream again about Old King Cole and his rusty nail. Their mother dreamed that something evil was living in the house. At breakfast she said she could see some kind of kangaroos with blue lights through the windows. She and Karen were trying to get to the other side of the house. "Friday's dream on Saturday told," George's father recited, "is sure to come true, be it ever so old."

Sometimes the whole family went to the movies together, and coming home, George sat in the back looking out the window at the dark buildings and wondering what it would take for him to be a real person in a real world of bright colors and to open a door and have something to say to every face inside. They called up the theater one morning to find out what time *The Blob* was playing, but they couldn't get through. The old building was on fire. They didn't know it at the time, but they were making a phone call *into* the fire. It didn't sound like anything, only a call not going through. Like so many buildings in that town, the theater had been struck by ominously precise lightning an hour before dawn.

They went to Florida in the spring. As they drove south it got warmer and warmer, and as they came back north it was still getting warmer. And then a week after they got back home, unless this was a different year, their grandmother came up for a visit, with her chauffeur.

It gets blurry. Green is a hard color to focus on. Something about the sex act. It was in the spring, everything was green, and

George was walking up and down the driveway, shuffling his feet in the fine blue gravel. Karen took her bike down the hill to babysit for Vernon's kids, but Vernon opened the door and yelled out into the yard.

"Don't you play with that person!" he shouted at his two little boys. "You know she's not your friend."

The twins ran into the house. Vernon had found out somehow that the family had stayed in what could only have been a segregated motel during the weekend of the Selma to Montgomery March. Then the next week their grandmother came up with a colored chauffeur.

Vernon got in his little blue MG and peeled out of the bare dirt next to his house and into the driveway, spraying tiny chips of that fine bluestone that stayed in the driveway year after year without ever having to be replenished. But after ripping out of the parking spot so fast, he didn't go any faster, because the transmission was broken. He could only go up to second gear. Slowly he roared out to the main road and slowly drove away.

As George passed in the other direction, he waved at Vernon and kept pedaling, on his way home from riding around and around in a circle counterclockwise, which was always the easiest way he could keep thinking about the world out there, the life it has, in dark rooms, or outside if it's warm enough, a place that stays awake all night, like the radio, even with the lights out, where it could be completely silent, but he would remember so many songs at the same time that he would be almost like those people he had read about somewhere who picked up radio signals through the fillings in their teeth.

Karen was crying at the end of the driveway, a long sound, a big sound, a sound to pull the family in around her, the way they always did when the cats were dead, but George was the only one there.

He didn't put his arms around her or anything. He was just there with his bicycle, the two of them standing outside the plain little cement-block house that Vernon and his wife were supposed to be fixing up in lieu of paying rent.

There was something almost liturgical about that crying, as if it could cancel everything, could bring the dead back from the grave, like Pepsi in China in that advertising slogan that did not translate well. They rode together up the hill, their bicycles heeling back and forth with each stroke of the pedals.

Or maybe they walked. Maybe they left their bicycles there, or maybe they didn't have them. It would have been the same crying. He was wondering if he should go into the house first and tell their mother what happened or if he should stay behind and let Karen go in first, crying, and then come in behind her with a sympathetic expression on his face and, for once, nothing to apologize about.

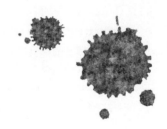

singing pumpkins

George was sitting with *Life* magazine opened to a page that showed Senator Barry Goldwater's face lit from below in the manner of kids in a tent trying to scare each other with flashlights. The sun had gone behind a cloud; he had read all his comic books twice; the foot traffic between the living room and the front hall had receded for the moment to the far ends of George's grandmother's house. Then the living room brightened, and George looked up from his magazine to see that his grandmother had burst into flames.

He sat there, staring into a pattern of light as yellow as the fire he would have drawn with a crayon, if he had not outgrown crayons a year or two before. The fancy quartz-weighted cigarette lighters that his grandmother had been filling stood beside her on the table.

He stared and stared. Those few seconds moved so slowly that already he seemed to be remembering this moment from years in the future, the way he would remember all the other moments in and near this over-insulated house—the icy wisps of vapor that a carton of Sealtest ice cream gave off when it was lifted out of the deep freeze, the virginal white gloss of bowling pins the machine has just set up, or the moment, best on a weekday, when the car would dip down the long ramp to the amusement park, passing through that freakishly ordinary buffer land that exists wherever normal territory borders on amusement park territory.

George's grandmother shouted, "*Matilda!*" and bunched the fabric of her dress together. The flames went out. Only after the fire was out and the maid had hurried in and George's mouth had closed did he begin to think how strange it was that he was already wondering whether the day's trip to the amusement park would be canceled or if anybody else would agree with him that only a family of cowards would postpone a trip to the amusement park because their grandmother had been on fire for three seconds.

The next few minutes could best be described as the bustle in a house the moment after someone has been harmlessly on fire. The sun came out, shining through a cut glass punch bowl, throwing spots of light, tricolored like grains of candy corn, across the wallpaper. People came and went around George's grandmother's chair, bringing her various-sized glasses of water, which she placed on the table beside the cigarette lighters.

* * *

If you don't know what year it was when something happened, you don't know much—which is why smart people always write the date and location on the back of their snapshots. There is a chance that George remembered everything wrong, that he was reading nothing, that it was actually Easter Sunday, and the amusement park was closed for the season.

Perhaps he was really hoping that they could go bowling. As he sat there across from his grandmother, with or without a magazine, his eyes would have already been warmed by the thought of the red-and-white marbling of the undrilled, grapefruit-size duckpin balls. Perhaps this was the day of his yearly argument with his parents about whether or not people in polite society ever went bowling on Easter Sunday.

* * *

Across the Potomac from the amusement park, you could have crawled up out of the water, into the same riparian thickness of woods as on the Maryland side, and been arrested. It is wonderful to think how close the southernmost curve of the roller-coaster came to the headquarters of the CIA, its location not yet officially acknowledged—just the distance of a shout across the river into a hundred hard-windowed offices. It is wonderful to think how easily the world could have blown up—and if it had, it would have happened there—how that reach of hills and water might have blinked into flame any afternoon, how the faces of families coming down the ramp toward the parking lot might have been daguerreotyped forever against their black windshields, never to reach the park but always to love that tall, white-painted machinery coming into view over the trees.

* * *

On an afternoon when he hadn't seen the Potomac for years, when he had flown from Denver into the capital for a meeting of the American Association of Private Business Schools, George ran into a friend from a previous job who talked him into going to look at some silk screen exhibits at what used to be the amusement park, converted now into an art center. They rode the metro bus north, past the place in Rock Creek Park where the stream ran over the paved road in the only true ford he'd ever seen, where his grandparents could actually drive through the water in their Cadillac, and farther north, past the mausoleum where both of them were now shelved aboveground forever.

Graphics galleries had established themselves around the base of what used to be the airplane ride. Tubes of pink light spelled out "PRINTS ETC" and "GLASS DAFFODIL." George's friend Dave stood looking at the paintings while George wandered around outside.

He tried to remember the noise that had once filled this place on a weekday—small steps on the contoured blacktop, the clatter and squeak of machinery, the muffled voices of children who have enough tickets for several rides—but it kept getting mixed up with something closer to home, the sound of the miniature amusement park that had been installed in his local Megasavers Plus supermarket. There, opposite the video department and not far from the bank and the limited-hours post office, stood a cluster of Nintendo games, a two-seat Ferris wheel, a coin-operated train ride that circled among shocks of corn, and a computer-operated puppet stage. The only kids George had ever seen playing those games were so young that they didn't seem to know whether their parents had put a quarter in or not; they just slammed their hands against the buttons with their mouths open.

On the puppet stage, overlooking the video games, stood the members of "Farmer Joe's Happy Hoedown," which consisted of several life-size mechanical figures: a farmer and his wife with pumpkins for heads, and their helpers, including a hen whose eyeballs could move back and forth behind glamorous eyelashes and a donkey with long ears peeking out through holes cut in a straw hat.

When they sang their song, the hinged mouth in Farmer Joe's pumpkin head was supposed to open and close, and his helpers were supposed to move around and jiggle their pitchforks while a patch of smiling radishes sprang from the ground and swayed back and forth to the beat of the song. But for months, at least for as long as George had been going there, the computer that synchronized the mechanical figures with the music had been down. The store manager had put up a sign that said, "Farmer Joe and his farmhands worked so hard last week picking delicious Megasavers broccoli that they got too tired to move around. We hope you like their show anyway."

So every three minutes the figures would stand motionless and sing their song, which began with a few verses of rap lyrics, complete with a bass rhythm so deep that you couldn't tell if it was coming from the stage or from one of the boom cars that often cruised the parking lot. This was followed by a chorus so loud that you could hear it all over the store:

> Be a Megasavers hero!
> You can have a ball,
> If you just say no
> To drugs and alcohol!

Mothers with their shopping carts would look around to see where all the singing was coming from, and in the model amusement park, the kids would slam-slam a little harder on their unresponsive Nintendo buttons.

* * *

Across the walkway from the place where the airplane ride had been, in a building that might have been the same structure that housed the Spook Tunnel, a framed poster in the window showed James Dean hunched over the counter of a diner. A tube of orange light ran along the rim of the counter, stopping at the point where it was blocked by James Dean's elbow. In the building to the north of the James Dean poster, mobiles consisting of a number of stylized wooden owls, finely sanded, flat as gingerbread cookies, now hung from the ceiling. This art center was really more of an arts-and-crafts center; George could even smell a whiff of lavender gift soap from a nearby door.

In summer it would have been full daylight still, and the trees would have been too thick for anyone to see up to the main road. Now he could see the lights getting brighter in the new subdivisions that had grown up on the uphill side of the highway. The houses were very nice, but they all faced away from the main road, the way houses turn away from a railroad track, showing rear walls and kitchen vents as faceless as the delivery entrance to a restaurant.

As the lights got brighter around him, George could see that almost every shop in the whole art center had one of those illuminated posters in the window. One showed a tropical mansion towering above a five-car garage in which were visible the rear ends of a Ferrari, a Porsche, a Mercedes, a Corvette, and a BMW, their electric taillights glowing red—all this below the legend "JUSTIFICATION FOR HIGHER EDUCATION."

* * *

This is what happens when the world does not blow up, George was thinking. He was thinking and thinking about whatever occurred to him, because his friend would not come out of the shop, and he didn't want to go inside. This is why you look down a row of houses and everything on both sides of the street looks so dead: because it is dead, because actually everything did blow up, the way we always knew it had to, only it happened in one of those alternate branchings of time that science fiction writers find useful.

Maybe the spots where the two branches touch are the places in which fire is most likely to occupy regions of our memory where it does not belong, as in George's recollection of his two cousins in the recreation room, with the lights out, setting their fingers on fire with lighter fluid and making ghost noises. It could not have happened. They had waved their burning fingers in the dark for ten seconds, far longer than they could have in real life without being burned.

It would be nice to think that all inappropriate light comes from the same event, especially around this primary target—where metal halide fixtures blaze on tall poles in the parking lot to protect the people carrying wrapped serigraphs from being murdered outside their Volvos, where the tubes of light in electrical posters have been engineered to make drug dealers feel better about themselves—a place where people can bring their memories with them on the bus and take them away on the bus, however impossible they may be, however unlikely it is that anybody else's grandmother can be remembered to have had the same accident with the same tableful of cigarette lighters.

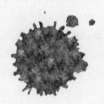

a foolish
but lovable airport

It is very satisfying to be part of a dialogue in which a man invites a woman whom he's already given up on to come visit him at his parents' summer house, at the very moment when that woman has a man in her apartment watching basketball and waiting for her to come back inside with the barbecued chicken legs. I leaned against the waist-high concrete wall that separates our two halves of the shared balcony, cantilevered over the smoke of somebody else's hamburgers being grilled one floor below, and said you could stay there as long as you wanted. That's what we always say when we invite someone out to be a houseguest, and we always make it clear that they will have their own room.

"Of course I will," you said, as I waited for the implied comma and the neutralizing counterclause, and when they did not come, I was not sure what to do.

It was the one day of the year when white fluff from some kind of tree blew in the air and collected in little transparent drifts against the curb. We both looked up at an airplane that was going over on its final approach to the airport two towns away, always the same aircraft, a homely, stubby little two-engine jet, this one painted up to look like Shamu, the Killer Whale. Then you went back to basting chicken legs, your back straight as a dancer's, the same easy slant over the grill, and I went inside my own kitchen, knowing that words pronounced in chicken smoke can never be wholly false or wholly true. In literary theory, a statement like that is considered mystification, but I'll stand behind it.

So at least I was able to slide the glass door shut behind me and go back to being a professional kind of guy, with paperwork at the kitchen table and a head full of positive thoughts on behalf of the category of houseguests, at all cottages, those important strangers on whose account we will hope for a good flight and good weather. I know how it feels to be resting from the trip, the long hum of a turboprop still vibrating in your ears, in a gingham-wallpapered room silent in the breeze through white curtains.

That's a nice phrase. I should have said that, instead of just looking up into the air and wondering what cute themed livery (*Star Wars, The Little Mermaid*) the next aircraft coming over on finals would be painted in. But that too would be a problem. People who work together should not accidentally live next door to each other, because they will end up unable to talk about anything but the airplanes that pass over, while one of them bends gracefully, straight-backed over the grill, using a soft-bristled brush to put red sauce on the chicken for the unseen person who has come over to watch the basketball players run back and forth.

Maybe I shouldn't have brought up the subject—though my experience with subjects has been that when you bring them up, it is exactly the same as not bringing them up. Maybe it's better just to think about it, about the word I love so much: *houseguest*. A houseguest is a privileged character. He or she does not need to get a preparatory orange tan from one of those radiation chambers that my doctor calls melanoma mattresses. You can get off the plane white as a potato and nobody will care, and you will have free access to as many sun-protection factors of sunblock as there is space for them under the sink in the guests' bathroom.

A houseguest doesn't even have to be perfectly dressed. That idea is a big lie of cartoonists. One artist in particular that I keep seeing almost every week sketches with fluent freehand lines sleek partygoers with oversized wine glasses, guys in perfect suits with the jacket fabric rumpled at the inside bend of an elbow as evenly as the pleats of an accordion and the bulge of a Rolex somehow recognizable beneath the sleeve. Everybody's hair is drawn beautifully; even the pattern baldness of stocky young power lawyers is perfectly rendered, their side fringes crimped and layered in the artist's elegant pen-twirl, and one of them always makes a nonchalant remark, which usually I don't quite get, about how rich they all are.

All you need to get you there is the word *houseguest*. That word will make a space available for you on the skinny, red, thirty-five-passenger commuter plane, with its solitary flight attendant rushing around through the whole short trip, trying to get everybody on the aircraft *beveraged*, as they say.

When a plane is scheduled to land, people meeting their houseguests wait in a kind of chain-link enclosure between the terminal building and the paved space where the planes wait, which many people inaccurately call *tarmac*, that word being a former trademark for a tar-based paving composition and now popular on prime-time news because the sound of it resonates well with that serious tone newscasters put into their voices when they are reporting terrorist attacks.

When the flight lands and the forward hatch opens from the port side, we look and look, until we and the other people waiting catch sight of our houseguests in the fierce light. Sometimes if the planes are running late and need to take off again as soon as they can get the outgoing passengers aboard and belted in, they leave the starboard turboprop running, feathering in the air, as if on the landing deck of an old aircraft carrier. Upstairs in the house, it is customary for an arriving houseguest to take a little nap, as the light streams through the curtains.

If the weather is all right the next morning, we go for a run—me, my sister, and my brother-in-law—down the ruts of the long driveway and then for a few miles along the sand road that runs through high scrub a quarter mile inland from the cottage. My parents bought this place fifteen years ago. I still don't know how, and I never felt it was my place to ask: a miracle deal, a left-wing realtor so radical that he or she doesn't even put the little copyright bubble at the end of the word? Incidentally, *cottage* is just the word people use out here to mean a house, of any size, without a basement.

We run slowly, in a close pack, and sometimes we go for half a mile without talking, in the bright haze over the rises and dips of green bramble that the road cuts through, with the ocean on the left, which you can't see except for in a few spots, and higher ground sloping gently upward to the right. Sometimes we talk about business—mostly his business, because I don't have a business.

What's weird about running at the cottage is that we only do it after breakfast, and it's always a serious breakfast. We trot slowly in the sun, full of pancakes and bacon and eggs mopped up from the plate with toast.

Maybe they make these meals just for me, because I'm the one who comes back for only a short time—the swinging single, with the beginnings of osteoarthritis in my tennis shoulder and a good enough appetite to fill myself up and then run off the eggs and toast—and after a few days I fly back home, to a place almost as far from the ocean as you can get in the continent of North America. I have no complaints; the house is nice, and they give me a nice room—not always the same one every year, depending on who else is staying there—but with everything there is to do, we all seem to spend a lot of time sitting around. There's plenty to read, of course, but it's hard to get started on a real book. If my parents ever see me paging through my sister's *Cosmopolitan*, they start to look uneasy, not knowing whether to smile understandingly or to look away.

I should tell them to relax. I'm just reading a magazine. There's nothing for them to be sensitive about. Besides, along with the pictures there are some very good articles.

So my sister and my brother-in-law and I all get up from the breakfast table, finally, and go running, with the ocean on our left and our stomachs bouncing in front of us, past Frank and Judy Rackoff's big house, where at least once a season somebody comes along with a can of paint and changes the name on the mailbox to *Jackoff*.

* * *

What can I show you? The light that we run through in the mornings is like a thin plasma with a current running through it at a voltage high enough to make all visible air radiate light waves, or particles, depending on which experiments you choose to perform on them. I've never performed any experiments, so I have to decide for myself what they are. From the high spots on the road you can see boats, painted white, far out in the water. If they stay in the same spot for a long time, it means they are catching something.

As the day warms, the truncated cone of the lighthouse shines brighter in its coat of washed white. With the sun still low enough in the east for its light to spark from the surface at an obtuse angle, you will see so many points of light on the water that, even though it makes you squint, you will want to keep looking at it.

I don't have any pictures of this, and if I did I probably wouldn't get the colors right. Maybe I should see if I can find a coffee table book about the place, a great big one in the reduced-price bin: a whole compendium about the place, starting with a short history and some old-time pictures of people in high-necked dresses and big mustaches, and then beautifully photographed pages to be slowly turned: moods in fog, the bright sun hats of town, October solitude.

When I think about that light angled off the water, I think it is full of money. Maybe it *is* money, the purest currency. Looking at the light makes me think about the famous short story where a girl is being yelled at by the manager of a supermarket, and when she says something to defend herself, the kid narrating the story says he can slide down the sound of her voice into another town, the way I'd like to slide down that angle of light into the blue gardens where those girls live, where people walk around with clear drinks in stemmed glasses and always the same faces and clothes from the same cartoons—Rolexes, accordion-creased jacket elbows, perfectly drawn tangles of hair. I can sit in a wooden lawn chair for hours and worry about other people's money, reminding myself that if I had a dollar for every time I've worried about other people's money, that very lawn chair could be mine.

Still I will not have a long face when I meet your plane. You will recognize the cedar-shingled main terminal of the airport from television, and you will find that as on television, the airport is a happy place, with chowder smells drifting from the café and a whole crew of zany but kindhearted ticket clerks who spend their time trading straight lines for punch lines across the lobby's tiled space, from reservation desk to baggage ramp, and at regular intervals get themselves locked in the bathroom without any clothes on.

If it's a nice day, we can go right into town and take pictures of each other, some shots looking up the slope from the foot of what has been called The Most Picturesque Street in America. It's not beautiful really, just picturesque. If we go someplace nice for lunch, we can have the waitress take our picture with either your camera or my camera or both, called a *xenograph*, a felicitous new word in the language.

Even in the less expensive restaurants, people are so rich that I have to talk, in a voice just clear enough to be heard at the next table, about things they won't understand, such as my theory that Robert Lowell's poem "Skunk Hour" covered that territory of the mind so completely that it has become impossible for intelligent people ever to be mentally ill in exactly that same way again. When I talk about that and related subjects, I can tell from the backs of people's heads at the next booth that they don't know what I'm talking about. Back home it's easier. In my favorite local restaurant, I can just use the word *effluvium* a few times, and people will automatically understand that William Faulkner is one of my major influences.

Whatever happens, even if rich people think I'm a jerk, the word *houseguest* will protect you. You will be safe, in waterproof sunblock, wherever you go, at the beach, with no bathing cap, hair sleek as a seal, head in the freakish Atlantic, which is another phrase that I would like to say within hearing of some rich people and watch nothing happen. When you go back to your room, you can just lie down, in a room filled with that private register of light that pours into a house all day, if light has register, through closed curtains, when everybody else is still at the beach or has gone into town, and all you can hear, or could hear, is the high hiss of wind through a screen and once every five minutes the soft clunk of the refrigerator going on or off.

I've wondered about the light around that cottage, and I still don't know anything. The lighthouse that we never reach looks like a little paper mock-up. When Albert Einstein thought about light, it was a *Gedankenexperiment.* When I think about light, I just scratch my head. On days when we don't eat too much, we sometimes make it as far as the little village that the lighthouse overlooks, which is where we used to rent a house every summer before our parents bought the cottage.

I guess I have to say that the years we used to stay in that first cottage next to the lighthouse were a stormy time in our little family, perhaps echoing the stormy time in our country, when people raised their voices at cocktail parties. One day Mom brought home ice cream and a box of waffle cones. I remembered what a kid in my dorm had done to me. I told my sister that the ice cream was sour, that it was so bad you could smell it.

She smelled it, of course, and I smashed it in her face, of course. Our kitchen became just as noisy as it had been the times people were angry about the Vietnam War, before the people who could not be persuaded that it was wrong stopped coming. Something about the ice cream made my parents so angry that they said they'd be willing to buy me a bus ticket home, but I didn't take them up on it. I make no excuse. At least it was vanilla, so the drips wouldn't spot. As I walked away I could hear my sister crying in the kitchen.

Poor kid. Never got to see *Darby O'Gill and the Little People.* Spilled her milk at every meal. Found the word *fuck* penned onto the inside of the woven cloth Sam Browne belt the safety patrol kids used to wear.

Now everything is all right, except that she won't go shopping with me, because I embarrass her by picking one shirt up from the pile, and then another, and then the first, and then the other. I don't know how she wants me to do it.

She should have smashed back. Then we would have ended up on a more equal footing, a level playing field, as they say. And I like to think about what kind of a novel a scene like that could be part of: a sprawling family saga covering a hundred years in the life of a cottage full of people who can't stop smashing ice cream in one another's faces.

That's the tour, most of it. It's useful to imagine that we started out in the daytime and that now it has become night, so we've been able to see it both ways. If you walk in the other direction from the way we went running in the morning, you come to a real road, paved with the same kind of blacktop as the space around the terminal building at the airport. It curves inland and then for a short distance follows the shore of the long arm of harbor water, where you can look, from the stretch of protected beach, across the harbor to the lights of town.

You're not supposed to walk on the beach, because it's owned by a hotel, a long frame building on the edge of the harbor, with beams of light slanting down from the windows, whose photo spreads you may have seen in *Gourmet* magazine. If you want to make yourself unhappy, all you have to do is think about the people inside. They are not bad people, but their lives are so far away from ours that we can visualize them only from looking at the skillful line-drawn cartoons in magazines—the calm faces, unwrinkled white pants, and the protuberance of an unseen watch drawn so perfectly that even under a shirt cuff you can tell it's a Rolex.

But I know better ways to make ourselves unhappy. Even from the road, without sneaking onto the beach, you can get a good view across five miles of water into town. The lights there will be full of so much fine detail that they will work on your eyes in a way similar to the lights that you can see sparking off the ocean on days when we go running early enough—except that it's different at night. It's much darker, and the sun is not visible in the sky.

It's beautiful, and there you are watching it, but what always bothers me about standing there, in the middle of the most beautiful place I've ever seen, is that everything you look at is beautiful precisely to the same degree as everything else. You can drive into town, and that too is beautiful in its own way: the better SUVs, like Lincoln Navigators and Mercedes ML 320s, angle-parked along the cobblestones with their big convex tailgates and spare tires jutting out into the traffic, and some good restaurants, and clothes shops open late, from whose open doors the saturated colors of raspberry and turquoise windbreakers spill out into the street, where kids are doing what they call "hacking around" and trying to get their friends to smell their ice cream cones, and girls not old enough to be waitresses in places where they sell alcohol, are standing, calm-faced, sometimes with a slight fringe of blue around their eyes, waiting in line for slices of pizza.

We have a family rule in town: no complaining about prices; you either buy it or you don't. If my sister and my brother-in-law go into one store I usually go into another one, which means that she's not there to tell me if the color's right or not, so I don't buy anything. I might as well admit that the thing that makes me uncomfortable about going into town is that at some deep, perhaps unresolved, level, I still want to smash ice cream in her face. Maybe I should—bring it all to a head. Maybe that's what I don't understand about being on vacation: other people do it so well, weeks and weeks, but I still don't know what you're supposed to do all day. Look into each other's eyes? Wait in line for the Sunday *Times*? Go for a walk? Play tennis? If I ever did smash ice cream in her face—which would be especially ridiculous now, considering that she's three years older than I am and her kids are already looking at colleges—I would be doing it with mixed feelings.

* * *

On the ocean side of our cottage a long flight of wooden stairs painted green runs down to the beach, through reeds and cattails so tall that you have to lift them over you as you walk down. At night there are so few details in the shape of the water, and the green bluffs are so much the same height for miles, that you don't want to go outside without a flashlight. Once I got lost on the beach because I tried to orient myself by remembering that our stairway was fifty yards west of the moon.

From the top of the stairs you can look back to the house and see that the good news they've just found about has caused them to turn on every lamp on the first floor, where my mother sits at a desk, calling people, most of whom won't be able to be there on such short notice. The big secret going out in all directions is that suddenly it turns out that the reason this mysterious houseguest is here in the first place is that she and I have been planning for the last three months to get married.

A genuine surprise; the house seemed to tilt for an instant, you might say—but they could have seen it coming if they'd been smart enough. I don't bring a bottle of Mumm's to dinner just to be a big shot. They could have looked in the refrigerator and figured everything out. Semiotics. What's in the paper bag and why? When I actually said it, it took them so long to react that I thought somebody was choking. As James Thurber said, "You could have heard a bomb drop."

Then my sister's hand jerked at the table and she knocked over her champagne glass. Every meal that poor girl used to spill something. Later it was nice that she cried, and she was the right one to do it. I've never known a child who cried so easily.

Everything happens fast around here. The green-and-white striped caterer's tent has already been pitched and tightened on the grass between the cottage and the road. It stands in the dark, a Faulknerian shape without color, stripes leached, or bleached, of their mint green, the whole blurred structure of it receding from our eyes, in abject furious retrograde.

I'm glad we have that vocabulary. Even if we only get to use it once in a while, it can't hurt us. *US News and World Report* says that the big corporations are looking for people who have done some serious reading in widely distributed fields and who won't scare clients away by not knowing who William Carlos Williams was.

But I'm getting ahead of myself. It's night, and everywhere you look, the big shapes of houses have their lights on. Phone calls have been flying around so fast that I'm not sure where we're supposed to be standing, or even what the weather's like—dark, I guess, having been that way ever since the sun went down. I don't even know how many people are here. I count one, but then I look around in the dark and get confused.

* * *

Soon it will be time for us to go, walking and talking, presumably about art and literature, with no rich people around to hear us and not know what we're talking about, back in the direction of the cottage and its lights, where we will find that the *New York Times Magazine* has been left on the screened porch. I don't know where the other sections of the paper are—probably stacked in a corner to be recycled. The magazine's pages are wet with the thin mist that blows in off the ocean, the unsupported half of the magazine flopping off the seat of a white spray-painted wicker reading chair. We didn't really get married, by the way.

It will have been sitting there for hours, in the moisture, hanging, bent in half as if partly melted, the newsprint damp from cover to cover and as flaccid as the clock face in that famous Salvador Dali painting, which both of us already know is called *The Persistence of Memory*.

the flannery o'connor
award for short fiction